A GIFT OF OLEANDER

A Gift of Oleander
All Rights Reserved
Copyright @ 2018 by jd daniels

For information address: Savvy Press http://www.savvypress.com

This is a work of the author's imagination. Names, characters, places, and incidents are either the product of the author's creative mind or are used factiously, and any resemblance to actual persons, living or dead, business establishments, events or locales is entirely coincidental.

ISBN 978-1-939113-32-0
Library of Congress Catalog Card Number: 201893303

Distributed Worldwide

A GIFT OF OLEANDER

jd daniels

THE FOURTH JESSIE MURPHY MYSTERY

SAVVY PRESS
NEW YORK

"Time is the best killer."

Agatha Christie

1

I closed my eyes. My head dropped onto my shoulder. Moments passed as the rhythm of the train's wheels on the track hummed its lullaby magic.

"I can't get the lid open," I yelled. "My supper will burn! Zen, get over here and help me!"

"Hey, who cooks eggs on the radiator of their car naked? Dang, don't lean in so close. You'll scorch your girls."

I raised the plastic whistle hanging from a yellow cord around my neck and blew! And blew! And . . .

Groaning, my eyes popped open. I felt my arms, my legs. Fully clothed. Thank you, Jesus! This was the third dream I'd had in the past month where I felt vulnerable, exposed. I knew I wasn't myself lately. But, hey! I was a struggling artist on the cusp of being thirty, an okay apartment manager, and a kind-of private investigator with no savings and a three figure checking account. I didn't even have a man on a shining white horse in my life who promised to save me. Poor Jessie. Poor, poor Jessie.

Blinking rapidly, still trapped in the fog of self-pity sudden awakening, I looked around the viewing car. Nearby, two women chatted while a couple played rummy in the brightly lit car. My shoulder muscles relaxed. All was well. Just an Amtrak Silver Meteor catnap nightmare.

Nothing more. Snapping my seat up, I placed my shoes on the floor and removed my cloth neck brace.

"Coming through."

I slid my leg out of the space between the seats. "Sorry."

The man and woman smiled and sat. He had a wrinkle-free face, swept back stunning white hair, a goatee and a hooked nose. The woman's close-to-the-scalp haircut made my self-cut red mop look as pathetically amateur as it was. She sported an outfit that I was sure cost more than my yearly clothing allowance. He hadn't seen sixty in at least five years. She was likely in her early fifties.

He extended his hand. "Hello, I'm Simon Hill. This is my wife, Beverly."

I told them my name. We shook and I emptied what remained of the small bottle of Merlot into my plastic glass. Inspecting my box of goodies, I chose the largest chicken nugget.

"The food was great in the dining car," the guy said, grimacing and shifting in his chair.

I gave the woman one of my best Jessie Murphy smiles. "That good, huh?"

"Oh, it was," Beverly said. "Lots of variety. Beef Wellington. Artichoke stuffed chicken. Shrimp scampi. Even the veggie medley was crisp. And Simon said his exotic tea was a perfect compliment."

I set down the box of tasteless, greasy chicken and took another sip of wine.

"So where are you heading?" she asked.

"A small island on the west coast of Florida," I mumbled.

"Wouldn't be Matlacha I suppose? Oh, I'm sure it isn't. That would be just too, too weird."

I noted that she knew how to pronounce Mat Lah Shay and agreed it was odd we were heading the same place.

Her eyebrows shot up. "Well, isn't this a coincidence? Simon, did you hear that? This lovely lady is going to Matlacha too."

"Did you say your name was Murphy?" he asked.

"Yes, Jessie Murphy."

"You have paintings in Bert's Pine Bay Gallery, right?'

"I do."

"Love your work." Then suddenly turning pale, he put his hand on his stomach and said. "Beverly, we need to go." He squeezed his wife's arm, stood and pulled her up. "Nice to meet you," he said with a thin grin.

I watched them leave.

Sitting on this train was an anomaly for me. I was supposed to be driving to my creative winter retreat. But I'd had an on-the-job fight as a part-time property manager and handywoman in Cambridge, Mass. with an oak door and lost. The result? Muscle spasms in my neck. Driving wouldn't be safe, the doc said. So here I was. I'd have to buy a cheap car once I'd arrived at the island. No prob. Lots of flood damaged rejects littered car lots all across Florida.

I planned to spend the trip gathering material as subjects for my art. A gallery in Cambridge had accepted a couple of my oil paintings. Sweet. Double sweet. I was fairly positive they would take others. I felt more

3

than lucky that galleries on the island and in Fort Myers had contacted me before I left Cambridge with news they had more space on their walls.

Except for the roof and floor, the viewing car was all about glass. Grey and blue upholstered swivel chairs faced large window walls. Curved panes above each wall gave perfect views of the sky. Many, like me, were using their phones to take photos and videos. A teenager hurried through the door and retrieved a purple water bottle from a plastic pocket ledge under one window.

I set my phone on the round table near my seat and glanced to my right. A woman, probably in her mid-fifties, stared straight ahead. A hint of startle radiated from her eyes when she acknowledged me. I introduced myself. Told her where I got on and where my final destination was. She said her name was Shirin Raab. I nodded and stole another look.

Shiny thick black hair. Thin tense body. White blouse, black pants. Scarf shade of lavender. Posture and body language that made me think of the mother of an old friend, one I hadn't thought about in years. The unwanted memories that flooded back to me were a mixture of good and bad, more emphasis on bad than good.

"I'm Iranian," she said.

I clinched my fingers. My high school BFF, Bahar, had been Iranian too.

She re-directed her gaze out the window. Selecting another piece of chicken, folding into myself, I did the same.

After a brief silence she said, "I haven't eaten. They made me leave."

Turning my head and pressing my eyes closed, I saw Bahar that last time before she, too, had had to leave. A lump formed in my throat, I looked at Shirin again, "Who, who made you leave?"

"The conductor."

I raised my eyebrow. I leaned forward. "But they made the last call. You need to go back and eat. Don't let him tell you what to do."

She gazed at me for the longest time, then stood and headed in the opposite direction from the dining car.

Just like Bahar. Unable to deal with the consequences of facing up, willing to be hungry rather than confront. What could I do? I couldn't force her to stand up for her rights. Go ahead. Wear a black sheet the rest of your life. Leave your friend. Go on. Get out!

Surprised at my sudden anger, I tore into my chicken.

The guy who took her seat wore a tie-dyed shirt and baggy pants. I frowned and wiped my mouth with the back of my hand. My eyes narrowed. Mid-twenties. Greased, spiked yellow hair. Our eyes caught. He quickly diverted his. Long fingers gripped the arms of the chair. Nervous. No doubt about it.

"Hungry?" I asked.

Like an unoiled lever his head turned. His foot tapped the floor. He blinked at me but said nothing.

Hmm.

Something was up. But what?

I leaned forward to ask another question as two young Amish or Mennonite women came down the aisle. Just like that, Yellow Hair stood and rushed away, taking the same direction as the Iranian woman.

The opposite door whined open.

A man with an official Amtrak badge attached to a blue band around his neck stepped into the car. His auburn beard appeared frosted with white hairs. Solemn, no-nonsense eyes swept over each occupant. A walkie-talkie filled the palm of one hand.

The hairs on the back of my neck itched. He raised the walkie-talkie and spoke in a low voice while I scratched.

Murmurs around and behind me became a humming church choir. I wasn't the only one who felt the tension.

A young man in a hoody and sunglasses clutched a cellphone while studying the floor. Another gal in a yellow sundress with dyed purple and black hair tapped on her phone, most likely playing a game as phone reception was non-existent while the train was running. A male in blue jeans and a baseball T-shirt opened a container of noodles. His flip flops rested on the ledge near the window about three feet from mine. A middle-aged man and a teenager held playing cards but now the game was suspended as they, too, appeared fascinated by the official at the door. The two bonnet-clad young women in long blue dresses leaned their heads together in conversation. One shot a look over her shoulder. Our eyes locked for a brief second.

A loud clunk caused my gaze to shoot back toward the door. The porter reached down and retrieved a metal-clad notepad from the floor then walked down the aisle. Each time he came to an occupied chair, he hesitated, studied the person, and wrote before continuing.

When he reached my chair, I said in a light-hearted, ditzy-girl voice, "What's up, Cap?"

Funny how this tone sometimes encouraged people to say something that they might not have said to a more serious person. Funny how I felt I needed that tone just now.

Rain, sounding like knitting needles, clicked on the curved section of the ceiling windows. A woman smelling of lavender cologne swiveled in her chair and watched us with interest.

The man nodded in a wooden manner. "Just counting heads, Miss. Our stop is coming right up." He moved away.

I plucked a piece of lint off my T-Shirt and rolled it into a ball between my fingers as I contemplated the situation.

The younger me would have accepted the porter's simple explanation—the younger me, that is, who had never worked for a private detective or sort-of become one. Since stepping into the world of murder and mystery, I had become more cynical and definitely much more aware of details that said "Be on the alert." Right now that particular flag was flying high. Rubbing the back of my neck again, I watched the porter until he reached the opposite end of the car. He took a sly glance behind him and disappeared through it. The closing door wheezed and rattled like a grandpa's dying breath.

My decision was made. I would confront the porter in the dining car. That Iranian woman had every right to eat. Good grief!! This was

America. I stood and started in that direction. When I pushed the button, the door whirled open and I stepped across the narrow slits. The tracks shuddered. I tapped another button and the second door whispered and whooshed.

"Sorry, Miss," another larger porter with folded arms said. "This car is closed."

"But I need to get back to my sleeping car," I lied.

"Miss, please take your seat. If you need to talk to someone after that, you can catch up with them after you exit the train. Perhaps after you claim your baggage? You be careful walking about. You don't want to damage that neck any more than you already have."

Of course the porters knew what type of ticket I had bought by now. We'd been on the train for over twenty-one hours. Because the sleeping cars were four times more expensive than riding coach, I had opted out of having a sleeper. Brought my own pillow and blanket. And in this case, my heating pad and the neck brace that the porter had seen me use. I was thwarted and knew it.

"But…" I attempted to look around the guy. He seemed more like a thick-necked bodyguard than a railway employee, as solid and almost as big as a steel garage door. I mean, REALLY! This guy's mother must have stuffed this bruiser with fruity vitamins! A scar above his bushy right eyebrow ran into his hairline. The seats behind him were empty. Even the vases were void of flowers.

He pursed his lips. "Sorry," he repeated. "There's nothing to concern you. Just go back to your seat." His body language said: Try to push by. Just give it a try. I'd like that.

Occasionally grabbing a seat for support, I swayed from the erratic motion of the train through the viewing car and to the next one. The quick, jerky movement made my neck muscles throb. After sitting, I swallowed a Tylenol, snapped up my footrest, and lowered the back of my seat. When you were my height, five-foot-eight inches and having muscle spasms, riding a train had its challenges. I plugged in my heating pad, switched it on and placed it around my neck.

Across the aisle the two bonneted women were eating out of plastic containers. Removing their white hats, they exposed a thinner layer of stiff white material that covered brunette hair. A second later they took off the starched fabric. Now their tresses were only covered in a small scarf of white cotton. Ankle-length blue dresses matched. So did their black tights and thick-soled black shoes.

"So where are you from?" I asked.

"Kalona, Iowa." The woman on the left kept her eyes on the floor as she talked.

I leaned over and extended my hand.

The woman on the aisle giggled and took it.

"My name is Jessie."

"Hello. I'm Teresa and this is Heather. We're so excited to see the ocean."

I told them to have a great journey as we settled back in our seats and I closed my eyes. With my aching neck, sleep would be fitful at best. Remembering the earlier nightmare, I was hoping for dreams less foreboding. I lowered the seat even more, leaned my head to the left and drew the blanket over my body. One of the doors opened and closed. Someone passed through. I kept my eyelids lowered as I focused on the sound of the train's wheels clank clank clank across the tracks. Counting from one-hundred backward, my mind drifted and I dozed for quite some time before a noise awakened me. I frowned and sat up, lowering my blanket to my waist. The Amish women were sleeping, but one had moved behind her friend and curled up across two empty seats. I half-stood and saw no one standing. Heard no conversation. Nestling into the seat, I pulled up my blanket, closed my eyes and once again dozed off.

Within seconds the skin on the back of my head felt as if it had been attacked by red ants again, jerking me awake. I sat up straight. Turning over my heating pad, I found no sign of offending bedbugs. I turned off the low heat and felt my neck. What I was experiencing, however, wasn't a burning sensation. It was a familiar itch—a potent ITCH, something like what you feel once poison ivy has spread across your body. My hair follicles were definitely suffering from an internal, psychological attack—the sure sign of a problem and not a personal physical problem, a warning that something was amiss.

Teresa spoke in a low voice. "Excuse me."

"Yes?" I answered, now wide awake.

10

"Did you hear that?" she whispered. "I swear it was someone screaming. But, it couldn't be, could it?"

I stood and looked around the car. All quiet. "Maybe it was the sound of the train's wheels?"

"Well . . . maybe. Um, when we get to the station, do you mind if we use your cell phone? We'd like to contact the friend who is to pick us up." Her face paled. The sound must have frightened her.

"Not at all . . . sure."

She thanked me as Heather gathered up her pillow and blanket and returned to her original seat.

"Five minutes to Orlando," the porter called out.

I had half an hour to transfer to a bus for Fort Myers. My bud, Zen was to pick me up.

I re-adjusted my chair, gave the girl my phone and began organizing my possessions. Pulling off my tennis shoes and socks, I replaced them with flip flops. I glanced at the young women. With heads almost touching, they were gazing at the phone with nervous expressions. "Do you know how to use it?" I asked, realizing how thoughtless I had been and how embarrassed they must feel.

Looking self-conscious, they shook their heads.

"Here, I'll show you," I said in a tone I hoped was kind, not condescending. "Tell me the number and I'll put it in and when they answer you can talk. Okay?"

Their reddened, relieved faces nodded in unison and Teresa handed over the phone and a piece of paper. I punched in the numbers, listened, and then returned it to her. As she put the phone to her ear, shrieks of multiple cop cars and ambulance sirens made my heart flip. I looked out the window.

Doors opened. Men and women in blue and EMTs hopped out of vehicles. Florida Hospital East Orlando ambulance doors unlatched. Yanking out a mobile transport cot with a maroon cushion, two men in white dashed toward the train. Cops clustered with Amtrak officials. Minutes later, the extended cot rushed forward, pulling along Beverly Hill clasping her prone husband's hand.

"What is it?" Teresa asked as she returned my phone.

"Looks like a man is ill," I answered. "Nothing to be frightened about. Maybe the scream we heard was his wife."

Teresa whispered to her friend while I grabbed my carry-on backpack, put on my cap and went to the rack where I'd placed my one piece of luggage and the pet cage that held Gar, my plaster of Paris travel companion and confidante. I had wanted to put him beside me on a seat, but the porter had assured me that too many people came and went. He said Gar would be less likely to be bumped and tumbled onto the floor in the safety of the luggage rack.

Many didn't get Gar, but to me he was like a genie with magical powers or a guardian angel. With him nearby I always felt safe.

The temp outside was at least forty degrees warmer than in Boston. Palm fronds waved in the mild breeze. The sky now sparkled as blue as a swimming pool with its pump on. A flock of cattle egrets lined the green roof of the station.

Pulling my luggage, with long strides, I headed for the station and the bus I had to catch—pack over my left shoulder—Gar safely swinging from my other hand. With the next step, the garage door-sized porter blocked my path. I hesitated.

"You Jessie Murphy?"

"Yep."

"I have a message for you."

I set Gar down. The porter handed me a piece of paper. I thanked him and he walked around me. I unfolded the note and read:

Miss Murphy, I need to talk to you. Simon Hill.

The bus left in less than half an hour. I glanced at the wall clock and compressed my lips, contemplating what I should do. If I didn't catch this bus, I'd have to buy another ticket and who knew what time the next one left for Fort Myers? On the other hand, this guy was a potential art buyer and one of my priorities was to sell more art. The diversion of time and money could be worth much more than the price of another ticket.

Decision made, I walked to the information counter and asked for the time of the next bus to Fort Myers (two hours) and the location of Florida Hospital East Orlando. I bought a new ticket and went outside. The sky now more gray than blue. The fan-shaped fronds of a Bismarck palm drooped low. A worker spread mulch around its base. Finger-like projections of one pale, dusty green fan entangled the fingers of another. A mountain of dead fronds overloaded a nearby flatbed truck. The guy must have recently trimmed all the surrounding palms and scrubs.

I sat on a cement bench and placed Gar at my feet. Phoning Zen, I told her my arrival would be later than expected. She didn't hide her disappointment. I pocketed my phone. As the train rolled away, I pulled a bottle of water out of my bag and swallowed half of it. I recapped the bottle and stood for several minutes, breathing deeply. After collecting Gar, I hailed a taxi. I arrived at the hospital in eleven minutes.

2

I blanched. Simon Hill was dead.

Leaving the information desk, I collapsed onto a lobby chair. The realization that one minute you could be planning six months by the sea and the next minute you could be dead stunned me. I stretched my neck muscles and tilted my head to the right, then to the left. Leaning forward, I patted Gar's head for good luck. One never knew. I stood. *Live each day to the fullest,* my grandma always says. But what did that phrase mean, REALLY? Some days you just felt like doing nothing. I turned toward the entrance, thought of Beverly and retook my seat.

Less than an hour later Beverly, with reddened eyes, walked out of the elevator.

I hurried to her. "I'm so sorry."

Blinking rapidly she stared at me blankly, then burst into tears. I stepped forward and wrapping my arms around her, comforted her. She cried for several minutes, then cleared her throat and blew her nose on a tissue.

"If there is anything I can do . . ."

She sniffled and thanked me. I asked about her plans. She said she would stay until her daughter arrived on the next plane. Simon's body would be flown back to Boston right after the autopsy was completed.

"Would you like a cup of coffee?" I asked.

She nodded. "That's very thoughtful of you. You sure you wouldn't mind?"

I assured her I didn't. Knowing what to say in such situations wasn't exactly my forte`. But having another familiar (even if the familiarity was slight) human being present could help in a situation like this. One thing I knew, talking was always a stress reliever when tragedy struck. Keeping everything in was definitely not wise. I had a college friend who did that once and she ended up going bonkers.

The clerk at the information desk directed us to a ground floor coffee shop. I asked Beverly to find us a booth while I purchased the iced latte`s.

Beverly stared out the window into a courtyard garden of blossoming bougainvillea and oleanders. A woman with slumped shoulders wearing a white hospital gown sat on a wrought iron bench. I set Beverly's cup in front of her as I slid onto the wooden seat.

She turned her head. "It was dreadful." Her voice caught. "One minute he was putting his papers in his briefcase and then he just collapsed and fell across the table. And he's such a big man . . . I tried to move him . . . I tried, oh . . ." She searched in her handbag, pulling out a packet of tissues. She blew her nose. Tears streamed down her face. "I didn't know what to do. Thank god the porter was there."

The patient outside stood and walked down the brick path. We watched until she entered a door.

"I just can't believe . . . It happened so fast. He said he was having stomach pains, but he's always been healthy as a race horse." Her eyes widened. "Do you think it's my fault? Oh god, I should have listened. Oh, dear, if I had only listened." Her sobs were deep. Resounding.

I patted her hand and asked, "Do you have someplace to stay tonight?"

She nodded. "My daughter found me a room at a nearby hotel. She'd be in by ten. But, thank you."

Minutes later, thinking Beverly was too distraught to order Uber, I did it for her.

After she entered the vehicle, we exchanged phone numbers. I couldn't help but wonder what had caused Simon Hill's death. A shame that someone as healthy as a race horse could die suddenly. But, it happened. It was time for me to continue my journey. I looked forward to seeing Zen and all my old buds in Matlacha. I didn't suppose I would hear again from Beverly Hill and I didn't feel that Simon Hill's death was any of my business. Perhaps the urgency in the note only meant that he had wanted to commission a painting for his wife. Who knows? Whatever he had thought was urgent would be buried with him. After all, Simon Hill hadn't been murdered, had he?

The skin on the nape of my neck began to bug me again. Not a good sign. Not a good sign at all.

3

I'd taken the Florida Express Greyhound from Lynx Central Station. It was an almost six hour trip with a one hour and thirty minute transfer. The bus went through Lakeland, Tampa, Sarasota, and Port Charlotte before reaching Fort Myers as its seventh stop. I'd been unable to sleep. I was bushed to the max. I stepped off the bus, holding Gar's travel cage. The driver had already unloaded my bag. Thanking and tipping him, I looked around. No Zen. I shrugged.

The terminal was newer and better taken care of than most bus stations I'd been in. Tiled floors were clean and free of chips. Maroon-colored metal chairs and benches inside and gold ones outside looked as if someone wiped them down regularly. Two African-American attendants wearing black vests and black pants chatted and laughed with each other as I entered the building. I took a right and withdrew two hundred dollars from an ATM machine. Then passing a cop, returned outside through automated, folding doors.

The turquoise, yellow and blue color scheme of the exterior reminded me I was in Florida. As did the eighty degree November weather and the smell of the not-so-distant Caloosahatchee River. Although there were several signs posted that said no smoking was permitted, a cigarette butt was jammed into the cracks between the poured cement squares at my feet. I faced the police station, settling Gar beside me. The sound of running feet made me turn. I smiled.

"Wow!" Zen said, out-of-breath. "It's great to see you! Gator was going to come too until he heard how close this was to the cop station."

I laughed and took in my friend: Laughing eyes. Half-moon smile. Thick shoulder-length brunette hair. Snake tat wiggling and hissing on upper arm. Belly rolls protruding from cut-off shorts. Bling-empowered flip flops. Ah, so good to be back in Florida World.

"Sorry I'm late. The drawbridge was up. Here, give me Gar. Hi guy, you been good? How was the train ride? I always wanted to take that train. Could you sleep? Were the seats comfortable? How was the food? Did you meet lots of cool people? Don't even mention the bus trip, those I know about."

I laughed again. Good ole Zen. Giving me no time to answer, she continued to pepper me with questions as we strolled to the parking lot. I began to feel like an over-seasoned breakfast egg–but a happy egg–for sure.

Zen set Gar on the cluttered back seat. "I been wracking my pea brain and I still can't figure out why you carry this ugly (Well, he is! Don't get all huffy on me!) yard art critter around. He's heavy. You treat him like a pet. What is it? He have magical powers or somethin`?" Zen hurried to the back of the car.

I joined her and let her ramble.

Zen opened her trunk, shoved over a twenty-four pack of water bottles and a beach towel then tossed in my bag. "Don't worry, your painting supplies are safe and sound in my closet. You didn't worry about them, right? Why would you? You think I'm reliable, right? Hey, did you hear about the Nile crocs captured near Miami? Do you know they're more harmful to humans than Burmese pythons?"

Zen's babble didn't stop as we drove down Martin Luther King Boulevard and took a right onto Highway 41. Bridge traffic was light. I rolled down my window and watched the boats on the wide river.

"Nice to be back?" Zen asked.

"Hmm."

She smiled and started another round of questions. I put back my head and closed my eyes and her voice became a distant drone. We had just reached Pine Island Road when my laughing monkey ringtone went off. I slid my phone out of my pocket. Hm. Beverly Hill. Already?

I sighed, hoping she wasn't one of those needy people who had no boundaries. I said hello and let her talk. The preliminary autopsy was in: Simon had been poisoned. I listened as Beverly expressed her shock. Before ending the call, I assured her that she could phone at any time. But, in truth, I hoped she'd find another shoulder to lean on. She was a stranger after all.

"What was that all about?"

I told Zen all I knew, which wasn't much.

"Too bad," she said, "the death didn't happen in Matlacha. If it had, that woman would be asking for our help. I could use some extra money."

"Hey, it could have been accidental poisoning."

Zen started the engine and gave me a sideways glance. "I have a feelin' it wasn't. You ever ask yourself why murder seems to follow you around like a pet gator?"

4

Zen dropped me off at the Bridgewater Inn. "Listen, I can't come in. Got an appointment. See you in a couple of hours."

"You'll know where I am."

The inn was familiar territory. This was my fourth season to return. I liked the fact that I knew the manager—that the chairs and curtains and bedspreads were still the same. Although I'd discovered I craved new environments, if I returned somewhere, a little familiarity went a long way to making me feel centered. Like a tree, I needed sunshine, water and decent soil to flourish.

The manager greeted me with a warm smile and handed me a key as she talked on a phone. "Same room," she mouthed.

With no cooler or paint supplies to unpack, getting settled was done in a jiffy. Leaving Gar on the nightstand, I stepped outside and went to the railing to inhale the pungent salt air. Pelicans soared close to the surface, swept upward and landed on the drawbridge railing. Men and women stood on the bridge, fishing poles in hands. One waved. I waved back. Vehicles looking like toy tortoises trudged by on the narrow, too-busy, two-lane Pine Island Road.

I was in Matlacha—a rough-around-the-edges seaside destination that had no beach and only one short sidewalk. A place where three-story mansions towered over bungalows. A place where a person who lived in a high-rise in Manhattan wouldn't even consider stopping.

I didn't have to own a house to feel at home among the pastel and brightly painted art and craft galleries, candy and ice cream stores, bait shops, spa, restaurants and bars, realty offices or post office that made up the town center. The funk, true contemporary down-home funk, pricked my imaginative brain cells, drawing me back each year.

Tapping the railing, I strolled down the narrow deck that led to the front of the inn and road. I had an hour before Zen would return and I could retrieve my painting supplies. I turned toward the bridge. A weather-worn, broad shouldered man in cut-off jeans, a white muscle-shirt and a cap pointed toward the water. "Dolphin," he said. "Four of `em."

I rubbed my neck and watched the mammals rise and disappear for several minutes, left the bridge and headed toward Bert's Pine Bay Gallery. Climbing the steps, I opened the door and found the manager, an intelligent, efficient woman of about forty-five, behind the counter. "Hey, Cordelia."

We exchanged pleasantries before Cordelia said, "Oh, and we sold two of your paintings. The bookkeeper asked for your northern address, but I told her to wait on that. I knew you'd be here soon. Hope you don't mind?"

"That's more than fine. Got any idea who bought them?"

"A seasonal. If I remember right, his name was Simon Hill."

Blood rushed from my face. Way too weird. Way too coincidental.

23

Cordelia stepped forward. "Hey, you look like someone walked over your grave."

"Wow! That's totally bizarre. You sure of his name? Was he an older guy with great white hair?"

"Yeah, that's him. Package went to Boston. I mailed it myself. So, you know him?"

"If it's who I think it is," I said, "the right verb would be "knew.""

Cordelia raised her hand to her chest. "Oh! Sorry. He died?"

"Poisoned."

"Accidental?"

"Not sure."

"Whoa! You're right. Absolutely too weird for words."

I nodded.

A customer approached the counter to pay for a purchase. I stepped to the side. When she left, I asked if Cordelia knew anyone who might know the Hills.

"My helper, Alison, has a cousin who cleans for her during season. She'll be in within the hour."

I told Cordelia I'd continue my walk and would stop in on the way back to the inn.

Alison was unwrapping a box of Florida-style Christmas ornaments when I returned.

"Hi, Jessie, welcome back." She held up a pink flamingo sporting a red Santa hat.

"Thanks. Hey, what's with the protest? There must be thirty people out there with placards attempting to stop traffic at the bridge."

"Oh, they're riled up about the possibility of annexation. People are really miffed at Cape Coral. Hey, Alison, said you were asking about the Hills. I can't believe Simon Hill is dead. You investigating?"

"Not really. it could have been an accidental poisoning. I met them on the train coming down here and you know me, can't stop myself from asking questions."

"Oh, sure. I get it. I remember my cousin saying they were real nice people. They, well, I guess *she* now, owns the three-story job at the end of Geary. Real classy—the house and the owners. My cousin claimed neither of them ever looked down their noses at anyone."

"Did you sell them my paintings?"

Alison pulled out another ornament and began unwrapping it. "I sold them to the hubby as gifts for his wife. I think for their anniversary. God, another murder. Dreadful! Simon Hill murdered. What a sh . . ."

"It may not have been a mur . . ."

Bam! Glass shattered. "Oh dear," the customer exclaimed. "Oh, dear!"

Alison hurried from behind the counter. "Here, let me get that!" Hunkering down, she scooped up the larger pieces of what had once been a dolphin statue. The customer hurried through the back door. I glanced that way and asked Alison, "Who's that?"

"Helen Lewis. Lives in Bokeelia."

Thinking our conversation just possibly may have caused the sudden reaction, I followed Helen out the door. She stood on the back deck gazing out to sea. Brunette hair pulled back into a ponytail. Hooped earrings. Perky nose. Oval clear-skinned face. Her fingers clasped the railing. Tears flowed. Her breath came out as gasps. To her right, a man walked around the deck of a shrimp boat.

"Are you okay?" I asked.

She caught my eye, then averted hers.

"You want to talk about it?"

"You sure of your information? Simon Hill—from Boston—is dead?"

"I'm afraid so." I informed her about meeting the Hills on the train and that Mrs. Hill had confirmed her husband's death.

Helen closed her eyes. Her shoulders slumped, then in a flash she straightened. "She killed him . . . the bitch!"

I started. "Excuse me?"

"He said she'd found out we were . . . seeing each other. Simon called me from Boston. He said he was trying to appease her with another gift, but something was different with her this time. He wasn't sure what." Helen's lips fluttered. "Damn!" Her fingers let go of the wooden rail. She turned toward the steps and without another word disappeared around the corner.

It was possible, of course. Wives did murder unfaithful husbands. But Beverly Hill? The poor thing seemed genuinely distraught at the hospital. Besides, if Simon was poisoned, wouldn't it be too obvious for Beverly to have done it? And if she had, why would she call me with the information? Plus, it really could have been an accidental poisoning.

On a train? Hm. What kind of poison, I wondered, had killed him?

5

Zen sat in a yellow fish-shaped Adirondack chair. Shoes off. Face raised toward the sun.

"I hope," I said, "you're doused in sunscreen."

"Always." She pushed out of the chair.

Zen lived in a single-wide trailer on May Street not far from a real estate office, a popular breakfast/lunch spot and CW Fudge. She said she was glad Chris Efron, the co-owner of the candy store had convinced her that fudge wasn't fattening, because she had no willpower and his words had taken away her guilt. According to her, the doc warned her that she carried around thirty pounds more than she should and she should be concerned about diabetes. I had encouraged her to join me on my morning power walks, but she just looked at me as if I'd grown another head. She opened the CW door.

"Well! Look who's here! My favorite seasonal artist and super sleuth!" Chris came around the corner and we hugged.

Chris was over-the-top handsome—broad shoulders, narrow hips, square jaw, intelligent eyes, long, swept-back hair—but better yet, he was a man content that he was finally living his dream. For him, being the Matlacha candy man was what life was all about. While he and I chatted, Zen ordered a pecan turtle. "Jessie?" she asked.

"Nothing right now," I mouthed before again giving Chris my full attention as he continued. ". . . and, he was one of my best customers. He sent boxes of chocolates to all his employees for every holiday. Why in the world would anyone want to kill him?"

Before I opened my mouth to protest the possibly false assumption, he glanced toward Zen, then readjusted his shoulder and in a conspirator's voice said: "Go talk to Breece Devino, he's a country singer."

"But, I'm not investigating . . ."

He interrupted me. "Just go talk to him." Chris smiled a broad smile at the customer coming in the door. As he greeted her, Zen and I left.

Zen took a bite out of her candy turtle. "So we're not investigating this death yet, right?"

"Not officially."

"No one hired us? No one has said he was murdered?"

"Nope."

"I don't know about you, but I need money to pay my bills. You independently wealthy?"

"Yeah, right!"

"So, how about we wait until someone declares it a murder and is willing to pay for our time?"

I shrugged and wondered how long it would take Zen's curiosity to kick in. My own snoop engine was revving.

As I walked into her trailer I blurted out Helen's reaction and revelation. Chris's obvious need to hide from Zen what he was going to say made me keep his conversation to myself.

29

Zen's eyes sparkled. "Ah, hah! So, that's who it was? Everyone knew Helen was seeing someone, but no one knew who. I guessed he was married. Too bad."

"Yeah, death is so final."

"Oh, sure . . . There's that, but poor Helen, she deserves a stellar guy. She's a queen."

"I suppose it's natural for the "other" woman to think it was his wife who killed her lover," I said.

"I wouldn't put much credence in Helen's first reaction. Had to be quite a shock."

"Yeah, that's what I thought."

"You know, there's one thing everyone says about Helen Lewis."

"Yeah?"

"She'd do anything for anyone, but she'd also be the last one you'd want for an enemy."

After dropping off my supplies in my room at the inn, Zen and I decided to go to Miceli's for their two-for-one prime rib special. I removed my neck brace, vowing to leave it in the nightstand drawer under Gar.

Miceli's was hopping. All bar stools, high tables, chairs and booths were filled. We opened the door where live music played every night under a Tiki hut. A couple stood and we scooted over and grabbed the table. "Hey?" a man yelled.

People lined the back wall.

Embarassed, I started to retreat. Zen motioned for me to sit. I did. She took her sweet time getting to the irate man. I don't know what she said to him, but he shrugged and folded his arms over his chest and gave her the shoulder. Zen returned. "I got privileges," was all she said before grinning and placing her arms on the table. A waiter appeared and we ordered drinks.

Four distinguished guys in Columbia fishing shirts talked in low voices on our left.

"Nice to be back?" Zen asked.

"Oh, yeah. It's like I never left."

A man, who had been squatted down behind a speaker, stood. My eyes widened. Yellow Hair from the train!

Zen leaned in close. "Cute, isn't he?"

"He was on the train."

She frowned. "He was? I didn't know he'd left the area."

Our eyes locked. "So, you know him?"

"Sure. Cool guy."

"You got a thing for him?"

"Yeah. But no taker yet. As of now, he's just a poker buddy."

I grinned. Zen was always on the lookout for another boyfriend.

He headed for our table.

Zen stood and introduced us. We shook hands and he sat.

"Breece, Jessie says you were on the train with her from Boston. How come I didn't know you were out of town?"

He smiled a half smile. "Because I wasn't . . . well . . . I was, but not like you think. I drove up to Jacksonville to check out a gig lead and my car broke down. Had to catch the train to Orlando. Besides, since when do you need to know my schedule?"

Zen did a poor job of hiding her embarrassment. Her shrug was slight.

"Why didn't you phone?" she mumbled. "I'd of gotten you. That's what friends are for."

"I met a guy on the train who left his car in Orlando. I hitched a ride with him."

Remembering the candy man's words, I piped up. "I heard a rumor that you knew Simon Hill."

In an instant, Breece's eyes transformed from simmer to high flesh-burning flame. "I knew him, what of it?" His tone exuded undisguised displeasure.

"I take it you didn't like him?"

"Nope. That man was not likeable."

"Why not?"

Breece glanced toward the stage, then at the wall clock. He leaned back, then jettisoned out of the chair and bee-lined it to the mike. As he faced the crowd, his tense facial muscles relaxed. He smiled and announced his first number. Several clapped, one man beat a rhythm on his table.

Zen gave me the evil eye. "He ain't got no motive," she said.

I lowered my eyes and studied the salt shaker.

"Jessie Murphy! You just stop thinkin` that this very minute. Don't you dare get any ideas."

So Breece Devino might, just might, have a motive to kill as did Beverly Hill—Breece obviously didn't like Hill. I guessed I'd file that information in my head in case a crime was proven and the cops didn't solve it before someone knocked on my door and asked me to help do it.

Breece's music was like a meditative candle flame. Conversations dimmed. Lips curled into thoughtful smiles. Waiters and waitresses slowed their pace.

Zen continued to look annoyed.

6

The next morning, a soft knock on the door brought me out of the bathroom, dental floss in hand. "Yes?"

"Miss Murphy, it's me. Shirin, from the train."

I tossed the floss on the nightstand near Gar and opened the door.

The Iranian woman appeared sensitive and vulnerable. Maybe even more so than when I saw her on the train. When I stepped back to let her in, she hovered near the door. At five-foot, with her perfectly wrinkle-free olive skin and jet-black hair, she was doll-like.

I motioned for her to take a chair. "How did you find me?"

"My cousin, Mahta, who lives here, knew where you stayed. I house sit a place on Sanibel Island, but yesterday I came to visit her and ended up spending the night." She intertwined her hands on her lap. Her white blouse and dark flowing pants seemed made of silk. Embroidered slippers covered her feet. "I have come to ask something of you."

Something about this woman made me want to understand. Curious, I nodded and said I understood. But, of course, I understood nothing.

"Mahta said you are an artist, but also an investigator of crime. Is this so?"

I swallowed the word "yep" and instead said, "Yes."

"I have a problem. Perhaps you could help?"

I felt myself go cautious. "Of course," I said, "that depends upon what the problem is."

Her delicate fingers began to quiver. Her eyes remained on the floor. "Do you remember when you saw me on the train and I said I had been asked to leave the dining car?"

"I do."

"I was quite shaken. I hadn't been asked to leave. I left on my own accord."

"Okay, and . . ."

"I saw a man in the dining car, someone . . . it was upsetting." She intertwined her fingers and seemed unable to continue.

"I assume you want to tell me who it was?"

"I didn't know his name at the time. I only recognized his face." She raised her head. "It was the face of a man who raped me and who watched my husband be shot."

The blood rushed from my head.

She continued. "The shock was too much for me. I was unable to speak of it until last night."

"But you don't need me. Just go to the police and tell them what happened. They'll see if there is enough evidence to arrest him. Your identification should be sufficient." I frowned, thinking.

"It was a, uh, robbery—that's what they called it. We were both shot, but I played dead. I saw them both. I will never forget their faces."

My heart went out to the woman. How dreadful life can be.

Her eyes flew to Gar and stayed there. "I can't go to the police."

35

I leaned back in my chair. "Why not?"

"The man I saw is now dead. I saw his photo and the story on the internet news this morning. If I go to them with what I know, they will arrest me."

"But," I sputtered. "I can't imagine why!"

"They will think I am his murderer. My cousin is adamant about this. She insisted I come to you."

"Who was this man?" As if I didn't suspect.

"Simon Hill."

My brain felt like a pinball snapped from one bell labelled Hill to another. I was definitely hearing that name far too often. I leaned toward her. "How long ago was this?"

"Over forty years ago. The men were mere boys—teenagers. But I have never forgotten their faces or what they did." She paused, then raised her chin and spoke in a firm voice. "I have every reason to hate him. The paper reported it as a homicide from poisoning. I was on the train when he was poisoned. Wouldn't *you* suspect me?"

There it was. The confirmation of murder. I didn't hesitate. "Absolutely, I suppose, but I'm sure you know, your guilt would have to be proven."

"Do you see why I need your help?"

Like, duh? What she needed was a miracle worker. Unable to trust what I would say, I looked at the floor and then at her again. She *did* have a perfect motive for murder. But I really, really didn't want to get involved in such a mess. Sometimes I felt like screaming, "Just leave me alone!

She inhaled deeply and stood. "I understand this is much to absorb. Please think about what I've said. Here is my cell phone number. I am staying with my cousin in the apartment attached to the restaurant for a couple of days. She insists on paying for your fee." She placed a card on the table. "Please contact me either way as soon as you've made up your mind." Walking to the nightstand, she patted Gar on the head, went to the door and left.

I felt like I'd been glued to my chair with Super Glue.

The poor woman.

That night the one thousand dollar 1998 Honda I had purchased via a phone call to a garage man I knew in Pine Island was delivered. Junker? Yep. Usable? Yep.

7

Feeling the fat roll above my cut-off jeans and remembering again that I, ole' beefy Zen, should lose a few pounds, I plucked a red hibiscus blossom and stuck it in my brunette hair. I glanced at Jessie's thin, long bod. Envy? You bet. I'd never look like that. Then noticing Jessie's more than serious expression, I said. "Okay, out with it. What's buggin' ya? "

"You sure you want to know?"

I snipped off another flower and handed it to her. She positioned it over her left ear, then sat in a lawn chair and faced me. We were in my backyard. My incense burner-shaped fire pit blocked half of her face from my view.

"Shoot!" I said.

"Well . . . it's just that if I'm going to continue to hunt down killers and solve mysteries, I have to get better at it. I'm already worried I've started my old habits again. I already feel sorry for the woman who has a perfect reason for killing Hill."

"God, Jessie. That ain't right. You always feel sorry for women. When will you ever get over that?"

"I know. I know. I need to become more aware of my weaknesses."

"Duh!!" I said. "Hell, I remember when I first started huntin' with Gator in the glades, he gave me several lessons on how to stalk one of those beasts and kill it before it killed me. Twice I almost bit the dust, but I worked on my technique. Seems like you might want to do the same."

"Yeah, that's what I mean . . . kind of."

I half-stood. "You want a beer?"

She shook her head. "You ever think that you slurp beer like a bear eats honey?"

I stepped inside, then holding the fridge door open, placed my left hand on my hip. "Is that a no?" I yelled.

"Nah, I mean, yes, I don't want one right now. I want my head clear."

Outside, I settled again, stretching out my legs. Jessie could be one ditzy dame at times. Like, who wants to be perfect at everything they do? Good god, what a waste of energy! What's wrong with doin` a half-ass job?

Jessie leaned forward. "I've been making a list of my personality weaknesses that affect my ability to be a top-notch P.I."

Of course she has. The woman loved lists. Although growling inside, I grinned at her. "Okay, out with it!"

"First off, I'm arrogant to the super max. This makes me think I'm more experienced and expert at being a P.I. than I am, thus putting me in unnecessary dangerous situations."

I choked on my beer and grimaced. What is she thinkin`? Hasn't she already solved three other cases? I frowned and wiped off my mouth with the back of my hand. "You been solvin` crimes in Boston?" I asked.

"No, not yet."

"Anywhere else?"

She shook her head.

I shook my right ankle. "Hm . . . Okay, so you *are* arrogant. Three successful cases ain't much. Yep! So, FYI, that little difficulty you got puts me and Gator in danger too. Next!"

Jessie gave me a needle-penetrating stare. "No argument?"

I gazed steadily back at her. What did she want? For me to lie? Hah! "Nope!"

"Humph!"

Humph? Hah! Had to wipe the cartoon camel right out of my mind. Cute one, though. Lots of bangles hanging from its sides. Of course camels are known to spit something fierce. Hm, I wonder if I could bribe one of my buds with some land around them to keep one? "Go on."

"Okay, Number Two: Sometimes I'm slow at spotting red flags that could lead to a quicker arrest."

This self-reflection crap was getting REAL hilarious. Me? I'm not one for self-reflection. Give me action. That's where it's at. Gator wrestling. That's my style. I finished off my beer and stood. "I need another beer. You?" Jessie shook her head.

I went into my trailer, unfastened the wire attached to a hook on the wall that kept my 50s fridge door closed and pulled out a bottle. Stepping outside, I sat again, raised my bottle and said, "Okay, so you're slow on the uptake. Next!"

Jessie narrowed her eyes at me, then continued: "Three: I'm far too kind and accepting, which leads me to be hoodwinked. I really, really hate that!"

"Wow, you don't know how many late nights Gator and I have discussed that very thing! He said he feels like stranglin` ya at times."

She pursed her lips while I snorkeled around my crystallized brain-cave searching for shards of patience.

"Zen! You're just agreeing with me. That's not fair! Can't you disagree with one of the bad traits on my list?"

I noticed Jessie suppressed a grin. Thank god, her playful self was swimming to the surface for air. I knew she couldn't be serious with me for too long.

I held a straight face, but it wasn't easy. "Listen, hon, when you name one thing I disagree with, I'll tell you. Got that?" I studied my beer label. "I hear tell that over-thinkin` things and letting` your ego have its way ain't healthy. Ego is like this way too dysfunctional, over-thinkin` thing in us we all got to fight."

Jessie pulled her cap lower over her forehead. "Now, that little piece of advice makes sense. Thanks. Where'd you learn that anyway? Sounds like something Grandma Murphy would say."

I couldn't help but blush with pleasure. "Oh, I got my ways," I said, circlin` my feet like I did in yoga class—first right then left. "Okay. Go on."

"And finally," Jessie continued, "I'm too emotional. I allow my emotions to dictate my actions usually resulting in situations that escalate out of control."

I raised my glass and gazed steadily into the sky. Wow! Please, woman PLEASE! I need a break from this INSANITY cell!! But gathering myself together with the effort of a mom who has the urge to spank her kid but never would, I say: "Anyone ever tell you, you read too much? I ain't read a book since getting out of high school. I suggest you follow my lead. With all these weaknesses it's a miracle you can even walk out in public without getting shot."

"Zen…!! You say the most outrageous things!"

Apparently we both saw the ridiculous side of our conversation, cause we broke out laughing at the same time as an osprey shot from a tree.

Wiping my eyes after hiccupping, I leaned forward. "There's another thing."

"Yeah?"

"Add "too damn trustin`" to your list. You're the only gal I know who can leave her wallet or cell phone on a bench in a bar or restaurant and casually walk away from it."

"Hey, that's forgetfulness, doesn't have anything to do with trust."

"Hah! For some—sure. But not where you're concerned. You assume that it'll be returned with everything inside still there. It's like you're testin` your relationship with the universe or with some guardian angel or something even more cosmic. The disgustin` thing to me is that you always get it back. Boggles the mind, that's what I say."

"Don't always get it back, Zen. Wish that were true, but it isn't."

"Well, thank god for that. Wouldn't want to think you lived a charmed life."

Jessie smiled and shrugged.

One thing that drew me to this woman was that we had some similar beliefs. I believed angels lived on earth in human form and that a Higher Power existed. I believed in the power of positive thinking and that you could manifest (think that's the word) events to happen. I'd never discussed the "angel" gig with Jessie, but I'd been with her more than once when she raised her head and said "Thank You." Obviously she thought someone was there, listening.

I eyed the fire pit. Should buy a can or two of Rust-oleum soon.

Jessie fidgeted in her chair. "I just want to be better at what I do to help make a living, be able to see and analyze details more objectively. That's my winter goal."

"What brought all this on?" I asked. "Seems to me you did an A-1 job with the earlier cases. With Gator and my help of course. You'd never have a chance without our side-kickin`."

"Well, in the past cases whenever a woman related a story of woe, I believed her and took her off my suspect list prematurely. I already feel sorry for the wife too and everyone knows spouses are the first suspects in a murder. Plus, this case seems to be evolving around more than one woman and I want to make sure I'm on target. I want you to help me with this. Okay?"

"Sure, I'll help. That's what friends are for, right?"

Jessie's smile was broad. She turned the bill of her cap to the left, interlocked her fingers and flexed them.

"Hell, anyone ever tell you that you think too much?"

43

Jessie chuckled. "I've always thought that those who know me as an artist assume my logic is nonexistent."

I pursed my lips. "Hm, I can see that. You *are* a SNOWFLAKE. Being too serious just ain't a gift you got, you know."

"Hey!" Jessie bent to the side, grabbed a pile of cut grass near her chair and tossed it at me.

I ducked, let out a war call and grabbed a handful of clippings.

Once we were both generously covered in green cuttings and stretched out on the ground gaping at the sky, I said, "Listen, kiddo, just follow that Irish instinct you got inside that damn fat-free bod and swallow that ego and you'll be fine. Forget the mistakes of the past. Learn from them. Live for the moment, that's what I say. And don't worry, me and Gator's got your back."

As if I'd been attacked by no-see-ums, I jettisoned to a sitting position. "Hey, you sure you don't want another beer? Beer makes everything better."

8

Jessie left as usual around nine o'clock. She always crashed early. Me? I'm a night owl. Came, I reckoned, from seven years of working the night shift at the hospital when I was a nurse's aide. Going into the trailer, I pulled out the drawer under the hotplate and withdrew the deck of cards. I glanced at the clock. Gator and Breece would be arriving soon for our regular poker game. The fourth person, Helen Lewis, I wasn't sure would show up. After Jessie told me about the death of her lover, I'd expected a cancellation call. But nothing. I thought of calling her, but realized that Helen wouldn't know that I knew what Jessie had said. Decided to wait and see what happened.

The screen door opened and Gator poked his head in. "You decent?"

"I'm always decent. Come on in."

Gator carried a six-pack of Bud in one hand and a bag of chips in the other. As he slithered to the counter, the door opened again. "Am I late?" Helen asked.

"Nah," I said, "Breece isn't here yet."

"Lookie what I brought?" She waved a bag of unshelled pistachios over her head, grinning like a cat with shrimp in its mouth.

"Whooee! Those are pricy, babe. You get a raise or something?" I asked.

In the next instant, Helen's facial expression transformed and she collapsed in the booth. Apparently, her entrance bravado was just that—bravado—she burst into tears.

Gator and I google-eyed each other. "Good grief woman, what's wrong?" Gator asked as I placed my hand on Helen's shoulder. The door opened and Breece stepped in. All eyes moved to him. Hand on doorknob, he eyed Helen.

"I . . . Oh . . ."

In between tears and heavy sighs, Helen came clean.

When she finished, Breece walked to the table and joined us. "Damn. That's a pisser!" he said. "I sure didn't know you were seeing that evil bastard."

"For months. Remember when I took the two-week trip to Boston in late August? That was to see him. His wife had gone to Italy." She sniffed and I tore off a paper towel from the roll on the table, patting under her nose. "He showed me all the sites. We . . . ohh . . ."

I didn't want to speak. All that was coming to my mind were not-so-kind words about Simon Hill. But I was not justified to think them. Wanting to prove I was special, I'd had a couple of flings with married guys myself. Neither ended well. Lesson learned. Besides, unkind words have a tendency to reverse like boomerangs and smack me in the head.

I reached for a wooden matchstick from the box on the table and used it to clean my ears.

This was no night for poker. Or laughter. Or sharing gross jokes. So, shortly after Helen made a clean breast of her story, she and Gator left.

"Guess we know now who she was seeing, huh?" Breece said.

"Yeah. Poor thing. She's taking his death hard."

"Waste of energy."

"Yeah."

"So, why did you really go north?" I asked.

"What do you mean? I told you and Jessie I was checking out a potential gig."

"Uh, huh. Jessie may have believed you, but I sure the hell didn't," I repeated. "Why did you go up north?"

Breece's eyes narrowed. He pushed up from the chair. "Guess that's for me to know and for you to find out." He turned toward the door, then glanced over his shoulder. "Bye, Zen."

I raised my hand and gave it a "see you" flick of the wrist. When he left, I smoked a joint and hit the sack.

I'd been smoking pot since I was about twenty. Without it, I'd be more of a basket case then I was. Depression ran in the family. Hell, I could never remember when I hadn't felt sad. A sad three-year-old? Oh, yeah. You bet. Prosac and marijuana were my friends. Without them I would probably never get off my couch. Gator understood. Had always understood. He was the dad I wished I'd had. Finally, Florida has gotten smart and make medicinal marijuana legal. About time.

I licked my lips and flopped on the sagging queen mattress that filled most of the room, getting friendly with the water-stained ceiling blocks.

Locking my hands behind my head, I thought about the murder. Clean the adulterer's gene pool, I say. Who cared who offed him? Good riddance.

The next morning I bathed (I dug my baths) and took my happy pill with my coffee. Plucking up a bottle of ant killer, I squirted a couple drops on a piece of cardboard and fitted it under a broken tile behind my stove. Pesky critters were busier than slaves building a pyramid. Their path led from the tile all the way along the wall and ended at a window sill. I squirted a couple more drops on another cardboard and shoved it between the metal frame and the wall. "Sorry, guys, you weren't invited," I said, setting the bottle on the top of the fridge next to my Buddha poster.

Around ten Jessie dropped by work. I'd returned to The Olde Fish House Marina as a waitress. My stint in retail had ended when I told a customer to get the hell out of the store for criticizing one of Jessie's drawings. Seems customers are always right. Yeah, like, hell they are!

"When're you finished?" Jessie asked.

"Three." I wiped off the counter in front of the small square ordering window.

"Can you come to my room then?"

I sensed that Jessie was going into or maybe had already sunk into her single-focus mode—the one that was almost impossible to crack. Maybe she was already focusing on the murder or maybe she was in that creative zone she talked about. Fine by me. I hoped she'd taken the job. I needed to pay down my credit card. I also had a major itch to get a 50-inch flat screen.

A group of four crowded around Jessie. She nodded at me, raised her arms and took off on her power walk. I had to smile. She looked like some weird redheaded, wide-striding, arm-pumping crane, high-tailing it around town. People loved seeing her, gave them something to laugh about.

I took their order and they found seats in front of the live music: Banjo. Two guitars. Female singer.

Slapping lettuce on a bun, I thought about Breece. So, I"m attracted to him. Worse things to be. Like trapped in a relationship with a guy who puts an anti-shock dog training collar around my neck to train me to stop talkin`. I'd heard about a guy who did that in the Carolina's to a girl he kidnapped. Least *that* wasn't me.

"Mullet's done," Davey said.

I carried the paper plates to him and he dipped up the fish.

"You want to join me and Angie at Woody's Saturday night?" he asked.

I gave him my back. "We're busy. Sorry," I said.

Of course Breece wasn't a killer. I couldn't be attracted to a killer! Shit!!

I handed over the plates and made out the bill, adding an extra dollar to the price of each sandwich.

The tourist in a pricey silk shirt and khakis, whose upper body moved erratically like a man needing a fix, continued to talk to his buddy while handing me two twenties. I gave him his change with the bill. He scanned the total (I knew he would be distracted), dropped three ones on the

49

counter for a tip and strolled away. I put the price of the meals in the drawer and stuffed the extra cash in my pocket.

The music boomed. A truck spit gravel as it spun right and parked in front of the eating area. A cat jumped up on the railing and gazed at me with such a look of disdain that I gulped. Digging into my pants pocket, I withdrew the cash, separated out five dollars and leaving the kitchen, went over to the tourists sitting at the picnic table.

I held the fiver. "Hey, listen, I'm sorry," I said. "I think I over-charged you."

Hardly glancing my way the guy waved his hand at me. "Good for you. I admire honesty. Keep the five." He leaned toward the woman across from him. "And then I said . . ."

"No, no I couldn't."

He half-turned. "Sure you could, little lady." He smiled at his friends and I walked over to the cat and gave it a thorough petting.

Little lady? Creep! The sucker deserved to be stolen from. But, that's not the point. Not the point at all. It wasn't only Jessie who had some bad or weak traits that needed adjusting with a strong steel wrench. I rubbed my upper right arm, scratched my nose and returned to the table, slapping the fiver down in front of him.

3:15. Jessie's room.

"So what's up?" I asked.

"Well, we have a job if we want it."

"Investigating a murder?"

50

"Yep."

"Who hired us?"

"The cousin of the woman who fears she will be accused of being the killer."

Jessie related the details of the conversation she'd had with Shirin.

"Wow! No wonder she came to you."

"Yeah. We don't know what kind of poison was used yet—but according to the news it's a definite homicide." Jessie opened her drawing pad. "Take a look."

The first page was a pencil likeness of a woman. "The wife?"

Jessie nodded.

The second was a strikingly good image of Helen Lewis.

I was hesitant to turn the page. I knew who I would see next. I flipped it. Breece. Very Breece! Spiked hair and all.

"Listen, Zen, we need to question him if only to establish his innocence, right?"

I counted to ten. It wasn't like we were in a relationship or nothin`. Why was I so upset? "Right?" I managed to get out.

No way would a relationship move ahead after Jessie got through with him. Damn it. Why had he been on that train?

I turned the page. Another woman. "The Iranian?"

Jessie gave a quick nod and cleared her throat. "So, we begin by questioning these people and seeing where that leads us. Unfortunately, Beverly Hill is still in Boston. I don't know if she'll return to Matlacha any time soon. But I can do a basic background check on her and have

51

Hawk dig deeper. If I have to, I can fly back to Boston, but we'll cross that bridge when the time comes."

My unwanted emotions were petering out. "What do you want me to do?"

"Well, for now, I'm hoping you could just be with me when I interview Shirin, Helen, and Breece. Having someone observe the interviews and talking about them afterward would be dang helpful—maybe would even keep me from falling into the trap of misinterpreting a suspect or a clue or worse, eliminating a suspect too early because I feel sorry for them. Make sense?"

"I get it. Or dismiss them because of feeling some sexual urges toward them. Don't worry, I get it. Don't like it, but get it. But, hell, I need my day job. We'll have to work around that."

"I won't do the interviews until after three. Work for you?"

"Yeah. And now?"

"I'd like you to meet Shirin. I called and set up a four o'clock appointment. "Okay?"

"Sure," I said under my breath.

9

Shirin's cousin answered the door and took us into her kitchen where Shirin sat at a table.

Standing, she bowed her head in welcome.

The kitchen was one of those painted white jobs you see in magazines while you wait in line at Walmart. Sterile to the nth degree. Made me want to take the lid off the pepper shaker and dump it or kick over the waste basket—if there had been a waste basket in sight. Of course it was hidden. I reckoned it was too germ-infested to be in this la-te-dah idea of perfection.

The woman had no disfiguring scars. No evil glint in her eyes. No odd facial twitch. Just ordinary, well, not real ordinary . . . like some kind of strange queenly shit. The kind that put me on guard.

I realized I was still irritated about Breece being on that train, not telling me he was leaving town, not needing me to pick him up, not wanting me to cut his hair last week, and being on the suspect list. Attitude adjustment, babe. That's what you need, I warned myself. Shaking my head of cobwebs, I concentrated on the woman's cousin who had begun talking while I was haranguing my pea brain.

"It doesn't matter to me what it costs. I know Shirin did not do this. We want the real killer caught."

Apparently Jessie had made known the hourly rate for P.I.s at her, er "our" level of experience, car travel (possible air tix) expenses, etc. I was hoping the Mrs. wasn't able to come to Florida this season. I'd never been to Boston.

"Yes, good, then that's settled," Jessie said. "We need to ask Shirin some questions. Do you mind if we did it alone?"

The cousins looked at each other. Then Shirin nodded and her cousin left the room. Since my mind had been drifting out to sea in confused waters, I hadn't caught the cousin's full name. Dang! That was low-level P.I. behavior! Jessie deserved better. I straightened my shoulders and listened. A notepad? That's what I needed. Didn't all P.I. sidekicks like Doc Watson carry notepads? Mental note: Buy a pocket-sized one and always wear a shirt with a pocket. Business expense of course. In fact, I most likely needed to buy a couple new shirts for that notepad to fit in. Yep, I was sure of it.

". . . I actually didn't notice him at first in the dining car," Shirin said.

Whoops! More conversation missed. I sat up straighter and leaned in close toward Jessie.

Jessie frowned at me and moved slightly away from my upper arm snake tat. "You have a question, Zen?"

Eww. A question? Sure. I had a question. Sure!

"What happened to the other guy?"

Shirin let out a sound like a train putting on the brakes. "I have no idea," she said, ducking her head so low I could see a mole stickin` out from the hair at the crown of her head.

54

Shirin raised her chin. Raccoon in headlights. Bam! Body splattered all over the highway.

Wide-eyed, Jessie and my eyes locked with a resounding, silent click.

The question had certainly hit home. The quiet in the room was so loud I thought I heard a baby anole walk across the floor.

Jessie's face softened. Her eyes shimmered with concern. Dang, there she goes doing the "Oh, the poor woman" thing again. I kicked her leg under the table.

"You had nothing to do with the death of Simon Hill?" Jessie asked.

"No," she breathed.

I gave Jessie my shoulder, making sure she could see the hiss of my snake tat.

Jessie let out so much sympathetic air, I felt the breeze on my arm. "You poor thing," Jessie said, patting her hand.

Tears flowed down the woman's face.

I almost smacked Jessie on the shoulder to bring her back to reality, but I feared she had dropped so far into the well of sorrow for this woman that the jolt would make *her* swallow dollops of Shirin's tears and Jessie would drown. Thus proving that habits are hard to break. Damn hard.

The sky was a solid baby blue—not a cloud anywhere. An osprey swept low, a fish dangling from its talons. The odor wafting across the water was as nostril-irksome as ever. But not as irksome as what Jessie had just done.

Jessie gave me a penetrating assessment. "So what do you think?"

"She's got a perfect motive for murder."

"Surely you don't think she's a killer!"

"I'm staying objective on that score. You?"

Jessie turned her face away from me. I could tell she was struggling with her emotions, or was it with her thoughts?

"You're right. I did it again, didn't I?"

"Like big time."

"Damn."

"That's why you have me, remember?"

"I was ready to totally believe her and take her off the suspect list."

"Yep. Saw that as clear as that pelican over there. What's the next thing on the agenda?"

"We need to find out as much as we can about Simon Hill. After we know just exactly how many other people wanted him taken out besides Shirin, Breece, and Beverly Hill of course and maybe even Helen Lewis, we'll . . . "

I interrupted her. "Maybe even Helen Lewis?"

"I'll amend that. And Helen Lewis. After this we'll have a clearer canvas. I think we should go talk to the Hill's neighbors in Matlacha and see what they thought of the guy. Make sense, partner?"

I couldn't help but grin. "We *are* partners, ain't we?"

"You're dang tootin` we are."

"So we split the fee fifty-fifty?"

Jessie threw her head back and laughed so loud that a tourist leading a small dog stopped in her tracks.

"Really?" she said through glistening eyes. "REALLY?" She raised and lowered her eyebrows at me, then said: "You're damn tootin`, Babe. We're sisters in crime!"

One thing about Jessie Murphy, she may be zany, what with having a plaster of Paris gargoyle for a companion and all that mumbling she did with her absent grandma, but she was clever as a stalking panther. And with her karate black belt skills and the fact she now wasn't scared of packing a gun when needed, she'd made herself a damn fermitable force to reckon with—a force I was drawn to since the first day we'd met. Plus she was more than fair with money. I liked that. Liked it a lot.

Grinning at each other, raising our arms high, we power walked to the car, me wagging my head and fat ass all the way.

A cowboy hat, that's what I needed. A bling-studded Stetson!

Yeehah!

10

I was exasperated with Zen. I mean, GIVE ME A BREAK! "You never told me that!" I practically yelled at her.

"Yeah. Yeah. I know," Zen said, running her fingers over the brim of her new hat.

"You'd think when I mentioned we would interview the neighbors to find out more info about Hill, you would have mentioned that Breece was one of those neighbors."

"It's not like he's a real suspect."

Right.

I pressed my lips together. "I'm not sure you should come along for this. He might not be able to talk freely with you there."

"Sure he will. We're just poker buddies."

I flashed her a startled look. "You sure you're not sleeping together?"

"I said we weren't. Don't get me wrong, I like him, we're just not doing it between the sheets—or on a table neither, for that matter," she said. "Isn't this the coolest hat?"

Did I believe her? Well, kind of. *Never believe what one is told until facts are checked.* Yeah. Yeah, Grandma. I hear ya! "I would of liked the white hat better."

"Not me. I'm partial to this red one—sets off my hair. Watch out for making snap judgements. If you'd bothered to ask around, you'd of found out the truth—we ain't sleepin` together." The hat was the same color as the pair of shorts Zen wore. With her white and blue sleeveless shirt, she looked like she was ready to celebrate the 4th of July.

"So the plan is to get Breece and the other neighbors talking. And not just about what they know about Hill. About anything. This summer when Hawk and I went off on a canoeing trip, he reminded me of one of his best P.I. tips. He said it was amazing what you can learn by talking. Ordinary talk, he claims, can allow things to slip out because people relax, when they do, truths are revealed and clues are dropped."

"Roger that," Zen said.

Breece lived in a tiny cottage. Army gray. Broken mini-blinds. Mildew-stained bent gutters.

"You think he'll be home?" I asked Zen.

"Just a guess."

I knocked three times.

Behind the door, something or someone bumped into something or other.

"Ouch! Dammit!"

"He's here," Zen said.

Zen and I tipped the brim of our hats closer to our noses. "Always wanted to see his place," Zen whispered.

The door opened.

To say Breece's eyes were bloodshot was a major understatement—like saying that a yacht was a big boat.

"Zen. Jessie. Come on in. `xcuse the mess."

59

Every available flat surface was lined with empty beer or alcohol bottles. Ash trays and plastic lids from cans overflowed with ashes and butts. Dust bunnies were so plentiful that I felt he must have a cotton wood tree growing in a pot. Breece looked far more than drunk. He was high. Didn't Zen see that?

"Hey, man," Zen exclaimed, "You need to open a window, this place reeks worse than a wild boar lot."

"Windows don't open," he said. "Painted shut."

I backed up to the door, opened it and set a big pork and beans can that was planted with what looked like herbs in front of it. Another dozen lined the wall, all planted with sprouting . . . No, not pot.

Breece stumbled to the ripped cushioned sofa and sat—his butt sagged almost to the floor.

Zen and I swiped newspapers from two chrome chairs and positioned them so we could face him. He held his head in his hands. "I don't feel much like visitin`," he said.

I revved up my charm. Not that Breece needed disarming or anything. He was so disarmed, a toddler could have taken him out with a sling shot. I looked around the room for something I could compliment. Hm. Looked again. Framed photo. Great. "Good looking kids. Yours?" I said.

Breece glanced Zen's way, then dropped his head. "Thanks. Yeah. Boy and girl. Seven and five."

"Divorced?"

"Separated."

Zen tipped her Stetson back, lifted her leg and draped it over the thigh of her left. Her body began to move to some silent musical beat.

I concentrated on Breece. "Breece, sorry to bother you like this, but we've been hired to investigate Simon Hill's murder. I'm sure you understand that since you were on the train with him, we need to ask you some questions."

At the word "Hill", he raised his head. His eyes sparked with anger. He targeted Zen. She lowered her gaze, but not before a wordless message of "anger" passed between them. I looked back at Breece who said, "I guess you need to, you being *official* and all," barely hiding his sneer.

Zen shifted her leg until her foot hit the floor with a loud thud. Her back did a "tough" stance thing. "No reason to be snarky, man. We ain't cops."

I imagined her holding six shooters and barely suppressed a grin. You go, Cowgirl!

Breece ran his tongue around his mouth seeming to clean his teeth with it.

High Noon in the Okay Matlacha Corral. Bam! Bam!

I softened my expression. "Now, Zen, relax. Breece didn't mean anything." I smiled into his eyes. "Did you?"

He blinked and scratched his right ear. "Listen, ladies, my bed is callin' me. What'd ya want?"

"First, could you tell us your full name?"

"Breece Devino."

"Born?"

"No, hatched." He grinned, then not getting a rise out of me, said, "Atlanta. I'm twenty-six, case you're wondering."

"How long ago did you come to Matlacha?"

"Moved here late August. You do the math. Spent a week here last spring."

"What brought you back?"

"You're kiddin`, right? I'm the only country musician with my unique style in the area. I'm in high demand."

I came more to the point. "Tell us what you know about Simon Hill."

"Nothing much."

"Ah, come on. You can do better than that."

His bloodshot eyes glowered. "The bastard had no sense. He insisted we should incorporate. If Matlacha decides to do that in order to stop the Cape from annexing those parcels out by Miceli's, me and plenty others would never be able to afford the raise in property taxes. And once forced to sell, we could never afford another place on the island. Not with prices like they are now. The guy wouldn't listen. He could care less what we thought."

Zen and I shot each other a look. "Go on," I said.

"Nothin` more to say. I despised him."

"But Hill was . . ."

Breece interrupted me with a snicker. "What? You never run into a major manipulator before? Cape Coral officials knew his number. Rumor had it that they hired him as the mastermind to buy the land with as little publicity as possible in 2012. Fucker! The incorporation idea he was

62

touting at the meetings was just a ruse. He knew no one would buy the idea. Hell, he probably was just waiting for us to start selling so he could buy more properties to make him richer." He glared at us. "Am I sorry he's dead? Hardly."

Zen's cheeks reddened. "I'd always heard he was an okay guy."

"Folks are usually surprised when they find out someone they came to respect is a money-hungry crook, especially when it's seemingly a goody-two-shoe citizen who gives to local charities."

"He gives, or I mean, gave to local charities?" I asked.

"From what I hear he donated regularly to the Hookers. You know their charitable work? People around here like, er liked, him. They think it's cool he gave all that money and doesn't treat 'em like shit. Well, I know better. He's, or was, I guess, a pig draped in lamb's wool." Breece rolled his head back and forth. "Can we continue this another time?" His request had the tone of a child begging for a treat.

"Sure . . . Of course," I said. "Just one more question. What do you think of his wife?"

He looked irritated, then said, "Typical spoiled airhead who values money more than self-respect."

"You been around her much?"

"Never met her."

"How could you make such an assumption without even meeting her?"

"Isn't that the type all these jerks marry?"

"Did you know what sleeper they had on the train?"

"Nah, why would I?"

"But you were aware he was on the train?"

"Sure. I spotted him in the dining car."

"Is there any reason Hill or his wife would have recognized you?"

"I've seen them around."

"So when you saw them on the train, how did that make you feel?"

"Mad as a gator in the glades."

"Did you approach him?"

"Started to, but changed my mind. I figured strangling a guy in full view of a car full of people wasn't wise."

"Nice self-control," I said, "It's really hard for me to believe you wouldn't be curious enough to want to know which sleeper they had."

"I don't give a rat's ass what you think." He projected a look of steely anger.

I persisted. "Okay, so just a few more minor questions. Where did you say you boarded the train?"

"Jacksonville."

"And what do you do to pay your mortgage besides being a musician?"

"I'm a herb guy with no mortgage. I inherited this dump."

"An expert on plants and how they can be used medicinally?" I asked.

"Something like that. I work for a guy in Arcadia interested in organic gardening and herbal medicine."

"That's cool. Where did you study?"

"School of Herbal Studies at Bastyr U in Calli."

"Did you work in the natural products industry at all?"

"Spent six months with Celestial Seasoning but felt too confined. Listen, I really need to get back to bed."

Zen and I stood. I thought of asking him if he knew anything about natural poisons, but at this point thought it was too soon. I filed the question for later.

"Just one thing," Zen said.

"Yeah?"

"Did you kill Simon Hill?"

Like a male iguana that'd been caught by a man with a pitchfork, he clawed at his greasy, spiked yellow hair, then stared at her steadily. "You have to ask me that?" Grimacing, he rubbed his forehead and groaned.

"Answer the question," she said.

Breathing heavily, he dropped his head back on the back of the sofa and studied the ceiling. "No, I swear I did not kill Simon Hill. Although, if I were a better man, I woulda."

11

"So do you believe him?" I asked as we walked away from Breece's place.

Zen glanced sideway at me. "What I believe and know is that Breece Devino is a damn good poker player. Damn good."

"Even when he's drunk and high?"

"Especially then."

"What else do you know about him?"

"He ain't worth my time. Never knew he had a couple of kids and was married."

"I agree. Getting in a relationship with a guy like that would be more adoption than anything."

"Damn straight!"

"Know any of his personal history?"

"Lived with his mom until he moved down here from Atlanta. Likes women. Hm, I guess that's about it."

"So what's your take on the annexation?"

"I've been out picketin' against it. It's a raw deal for everyone on the island. Everyone thinks Cape Coral plans to allow five or eight story condo units to be built next to Micheli's. Can you imagine what that kind of added traffic would do to the island? Nobody could get to their doc or to the hospital. We gotta get it stopped."

I agreed with Zen, but as a year-round resident she had more at stake than I did. I turned to her. "You go to any of those meetings?"

"Only one. Had to work durin` the others."

"See Hill there?"

"Oh, yeah. He was real vocal and people listened when he talked. I'm not sure I buy Breece's idea about him being a crook. He seemed real concerned about what happened to Matlacha. Claimed he liked the quirkiness, the edgy non-perfection and all. I remember him saying that the people in the Cape weren't bad guys or nothin`, but they were landlubbers who believed in progress and we were islanders who liked things as they are and the two things needed to stay separate. I dug that notion."

"What was the tone of the meetings?"

"Oh, people were het up. Lots of yellin` around the edges. Plenty didn't think such kind thoughts about the Cape as Hill. How the land purchase was made with hardly anyone in Matlacha knowing what happened really had people steamed up. As I said, it's a raw deal for us."

"You rent or own?" I asked.

"Own. And, yes, if I believed Hill was part of this crooked governmental shit I would have been pissed too. He certainly was singing a different tune. " Zen stopped in her tracks and gazed steadily at me. "Enough to kill, you're wondering?"

I didn't blink.

She tossed her head and lowered her eyelids. "Think what you will."

I let that pass. Of course Zen was no killer. As I walked, I thought about Breece. I'd say he was a non-aggressive, mellow, intelligent man who drank too much and took too many drugs. If he was going to kill someone, he'd probably use poison, not a gun or a knife. And I'd say poison was something he had to know plenty about. Except for that last bit, this assessment matched the one I would have given Zen whom I was more than aware was surrounded by a natural fence of oleander—a poisonous plant that grew profusely in the area. Hadn't some woman killed her lottery winning husband a couple of years back by putting oleander leaves in his morning tea for a month?

I sighed. I still didn't know what kind of poison was used. Hoped to get that info soon.

Filing that thought and telling myself I needed to do research on the annexation issue, I pulled my cap closer to my nose. "Let's go knock on the door of Hill's other next door neighbors. See what they thought of him."

The house on the left of Hill's wrapped around the end of the peninsula. Unlike Hill's three-story number with no front yard, it was a one-story tastefully landscaped home. I admired the native coontie plant (another potentially poisonous species) that flanked the door. A black convertible with its top down idled in the driveway. I let Zen knock while I made sure that my phone was turned to vibrate.

The woman recognized Zen and invited us into her home without hesitation. Wide entryway. High ceilings. Pool overlooking the pass and distant mangrove islands.

We sat on a floral wicker sofa facing her.

Apparently Zen and the woman (Allie) took the same yoga class. They chatted about how much they enjoyed it before the woman turned to me and said, "I admire your creative work. I've considered buying a painting."

"Thanks." I informed her of why we were there.

"It's a shame about Simon Hill."

"Yeah, it is. We've been hired to help find his murderer and thought we'd start by learning as much about him as we can. Could you tell us what you know about him? Anything might help," I said.

"Well, I know his wife, Bev, more than Simon. We play tennis together. She's one of those women who could be better at the game than she is, but doesn't put out the effort."

"And how long have you been doing that?"

"Oh, let's see, about seven years or so I believe. Yes, I'd say that's the exact number. We began playing when Jeff and I first retired and moved down here."

"What could you tell us about her?"

Allie sat in silence for a minute, thinking. "Well, hmm. She always seemed on the dissatisfied side. She's quite a bit younger than Simon. Oh, not so young that she's a stereotypical older man crisis-wife, but younger, maybe ten years."

"Did she and Simon have a happy marriage?"

"As happy as most." She winked at us. "I'm not a believer that most marriages are happy. Seems to me that most of them are compromises of spirit and desire. But if you are wondering if I thought she would kill him, the answer is no. Bev is not a killer. Was she beginning to think about divorce? Quite possibly."

"Maybe she woulda benefitted more from his death than a divorce," Zen said.

Allie shook her head. "Bev comes from a wealthy family. She doesn't need Simon's money. Why else would you kill your husband?"

"So you never got the idea that he might be abusing her?"

"Abusing Bev? Oh, I see, that would be another reason to want to kill him. No, Bev was not a victim of domestic abuse. Domestic abuse is a popular topic on the tennis court bench. Bev volunteered at a gallery in Fort Myers run by advocates of domestic violence. She was not a victim, she was a supporter of those abused."

"Have you been in communication with her since Simon's death?" I asked.

"Yes, we talked this morning. After the services she plans to come to Matlacha to recover. Apparently she's developed stronger ties here than in Boston."

"What was your impression of Simon Hill?"

"Oh, he was charming. Always willing to help. Before they left last season, we had a problem with the boat lift electrical wiring. He came right over and helped Jeff work on it. He was very handy. I remember once Jeff asked him how he had learned so much about how things worked and he said he went to the library and checked out "how-to" books. Jeff and I later laughed about the comment, because today people just consult YouTube. He and Jeff were boating buddies. He'll miss him terribly."

She paused, then continued: "Simon was also a good dancer. It was because of him that my Jeff finally broke his "I only dance between the sheets" stance and took me out on the dance floor. Jeff saw the light when a group of us were at Miceli's. Simon was the star of the dance floor, asking all the women to be his partner."

"And did Bev like to dance?"

"Actually, she would only slow dance. But you should have seen them on the dance floor. Even in casual dress they appeared to be in a ballroom. I always wondered if they had taken formal dance classes, but I never asked. Poor Bev, she will miss him."

"Do you know Breece Devino, your neighbor?" Zen asked.

"I'm not sure."

"He's the dude with the spiked yellow hair who plays a guitar and sings in the bars," Zen said.

"Oh, him—the musician. Never met him. Saw him come and go from the Hill house quite a bit."

"When they were both home?"

Allie's cheeks reddened. "Well, not always . . . sometimes only . . . well, only Bev was home."

"You think," Zen blurted out, "they were doin` hanky panky?"

Allie averted her eyes. "I really couldn't say. In fact, I've said enough, more than enough. Good day, ladies."

She refused to say more.

At the door, I thanked her again and asked if her husband was around. He was on a two-week fishing trip in the Tortugas. She said if he ever called, which she doubted—seems the guys liked to be non-communicative on their male-bonding trip—she'd tell him about Simon and suggest he call me. I left my cell phone number.

12

"Well, well . . ." Zen said. "Didn't Breece claim he didn't know Bev Hill?"

"Yep."

"What did you make of that?"

"I'd rather not say yet. When you get back to your trailer, write down everything you remember from both interviews and later, we'll compare notes."

Zen pursed her lips and eyed me. "I'd say you're gettin` better at his P.I. thing."

"Yeah, if I ever get my personal failings under control, I'll be a regular Hercule Poirot."

Zen giggled. "Oh, I just love that TV series. Christie was a crime goddess, wasn't she? I hear she's written a lot of books. Almost makes me wish I read."

She stood back and inspected me. "Of course, there are a few problems."

"Like, *what*?"

"You ain't Belgian, you ain't bald with an egg-shaped face and you don't sport no mustache to twirl."

"Oh, Zen, get out of here!"

Zen lengthened her stride and strutted down Geary. I grinned and followed. Zen began to whistle. A woman I recognized stood in the front window of the house on the south side of the street.

I raised my voice. "Zen!" She stopped in mid-step.

"I think we should stop here." I pointed to the left.

Zen lowered the rim of her Stetson and walked back to me. "Okay."

If she had been toting a pair of six-shooters I was sure she'd have hoisted up the belt as she spoke. I was glad Zen was taking her sidekick role seriously, but REALLY . . . Like overdue it, Cowgirl. Didn't she know that westerns were passé?

Again, I let Zen knock. The door opened an inch. Helen Lewis opened the door and stepped back.

"Hey, I didn't know you lived here," Zen said. "Didn't you usta live in Bokeelia? When did you move?"

"I don't live here. I'm cleaning. The owner is out. I don't think she'll mind, come on in."

The house was furnished in a large upholstered, deep brown sofa and two matching recliners. Walls painted a deep tan. Woodwork stained. Floors faux wood. Windows covered in heavy curtains. I felt as if I'd travelled back north.

A pine needle scent made me want to sneeze. I caught myself, but not Zen—she let go with a whopper.

"Bless you," Helen said. "Let's go out back and sit on the dock deck. Not everything can handle the heavy scented sanitizer Mrs. Coldwell uses."

We sat in rusty metal chairs badly in need of paint. The blue striped cushions were sun-worn, the umbrella tattered around the edges.

Zen pulled out a notepad and pen from her breast pocket. I started by telling Helen how sorry we were for her loss and assuring her our questions were mere routine for our investigation. She said she understood. I asked for her full name, her address and her phone number. Then: "So you cleaned for the Hills? How long?"

"Couple of years."

"Yesterday you were convinced that Beverly Hill killed her husband. Are you still thinking that?"

"Oh, not so much. Bev isn't really a bad person. It wasn't her fault that Simon fell out of love with her. I would think she'd just divorce him if she didn't like the situation. I was just upset, still am of course."

The odd thing was, she no longer looked or seemed upset. If anything, she appeared calm and matter of fact. Quick recovery from such a shock.

"How long were you and Simon together?" I asked.

"We met at Bert's last April a couple of days before he and his wife left for Boston. As I said before, he sent me a ticket to visit him."

"So," I said, "you actually didn't spend that much time together?"

She tossed her head. "Our relationship was based on quality not quantity of time. I know he was planning to leave her for me. That was obvious."

"He said that?" Zen asked.

"Not in so many words. But he was."

Zen and I stole a glance at each other. The sound of crunching shoes made us turn.

"Hey, Helen, you there?" a voice called out.

"Yeah, come on back, Brittney!" Helen yelled. Behind her, a pontoon boat motored past.

A tiny mite of a woman with a pleasant face and silver gray hair came around the corner. A long-haired twenty-five pound or so dog accompanied her. Luckily, my fear of canines only extended to dogs forty pounds or over, but I still was leery of all breeds. "Come on, Poppy. Helen wants to pet you," the woman said.

Helen laughed as Poppy leapt up into her lap as she introduced us.

Brittany smiled at Helen. "How was your train trip?"

In a quick, fluid move, Helen lifted Poppy high enough to cover her face. "Fine. Nothing special."

"Nothing special? Why, you planned for that trip for months! Come on, girl…out with the details. Did you get back at that guy who jerked you around?" She grinned at Zen and I. "I'm sure she told you about her revenge scheme—that's all she's been talking about for months. Brittany frowned, glancing from Zen, to me, then to Helen who still had her face hidden. "Did I say something wrong?" Her voice squeaked like a bicycle brake that needed oil.

Helen lowered Poppy onto her lap and gazed steadily at me. "Okay," she said. "So I was on the train. That doesn't mean anything."

Poppy jumped to the deck and dragging her lease, headed my way. To my relief, my monkey ringtone went off. Poppy stopped in her tracks, then reversed and dashed back to Brittany. I took my phone out of my pocket, and walked away as I answered it.

"Hello. Mrs. Hamidi? Yes, this is Jessie Murphy."

"You must come. Shirin is threatening to kill herself. Please come now."

"What? Oh, my! Where are you?"

"At my home."

"Just stay with her and we'll be there very soon. Keep her safe, okay?"

"Hurry. Please."

Rushing back to the women, I told Helen we needed to continue our conversation another time.

"What's up?" Zen asked as we walked rapidly down the street.

"That was Shirin's cousin. Shirin is threatening to kill herself. Come on, walk faster."

"She'll feel better when she hears how we have a strong suspect."

"Let's hope." I raised my arms higher and we power walked the rest of the way to the restaurant.

We knocked only once. The door swung open. Shirin's cousin looked as if she'd been struck by a semi. Her hair was awry, her long pants soaked up to the knees. She couldn't stop blinking.

"Are you okay?" I asked, closing the door and stepping into the narrow hallway.

"She's gone."

"What do you mean—she's gone? You said she was here, that she was safe."

"Yes, I did . . . but . . . "

"But, WHAT?"

"She can't drive . . . I can't believe . . ."

"She took your car?" Zen blurted out.

The cousin gazed at me with eyes the size of navy pea coat buttons. "She doesn't know how to drive."

"Then she won't get far," Zen muttered.

"She won't?"

"Of course not. Don't worry. We'll find her," I said.

We searched until two in the morning.

"Why do you think she took off?" Zen asked.

"That's what we have to find out. It's too late tonight. Tomorrow I'll talk to her cousin. I know you have to work, so don't worry about it. I'll do fine without you."

"Not on your life. I don't start until 10. Let's go before that. I want to know what her cousin says."

"Okay, sure. That'll work. What are you thinking?" Jessie asked.

"Seems odd she'd get suicidal after hiring us. I keep asking myself what's she afraid of?"

"Me too."

"Cops?" Zen said.

"Maybe."

13

"What's the scoop with you and Hill?" I asked, flicking a piece of glazed donut off my snake tat.

Thwarted on the Shirin front, Jessie and I were questioning Helen Lewis—this time at her home.

"Ah, come on, Zen, you don't really think I'd kill the guy, do you?" Helen said.

"Anyone's capable of murder. Anyone. And even if I didn't think so, Jessie and I still need all the information we can get. So, out with it, woman."

"The jerk was two-timing me. I wasn't the only woman he was seeing."

I did a phiff thing. "What did you expect? The guy was married!"

"I don't need no mother. Back off," Helen growled. "Like I'm sure you and your redheaded friend there are perfect."

I am. Well, maybe not perfect—but close. Jessie? Not so much. I didn't even want to think about what Jessie was thinking.

"Who was the other woman?" Jessie asked.

"Name's Moon McCain. She's my . . . was . . . my best friend."

"Moon? He was attracted to *Moon*?" I said, flabbergasted.

She sighed. "Hard to believe, right? Christ, she's older than me."

"Where does she live?" Jessie asked.

"She's my duplex neighbor."

"Like, she has sex on the other side of that wall?" I asked.

Helen gave me a hard look. "Well, it sure ain't sleepin' they do."

"Oh, I'm sure it ain't." I suppressed a laugh.

"So, other than the fact that the married guy you were seeing was diddling someone else, what else can you tell us about the jackass that would make us think he deserved you?"

I ignored Jessie's frown.

Helen tightened her lips and turned to her. "Simon? He was way too nice to his wife, if you asked me. Kept givin' her expensive gifts. Told me once he wished he'd paid attention to his brother's advice. He'd warned him to not marry her—said she was just after his money."

Jessie and I looked at each other. Hadn't we just heard that Beverly Hill was the wealthy one? Someone was quite the storyteller.

"Got any idea where this brother lives?" Jessie asked.

Helen cringed. Her shoulders slumped even further. "In Boston somewhere. Not sure where. Think they had a fallin' out or somethin'."

"Do you know if the jerk had any enemies—besides you, I assume— and maybe his wife," I asked. Eyeing Helen, who was starting to act real nervous, I scratched at my thumbnail.

"I know he got some phone calls he didn't like. They usta make him real mad, but other than that I can't think of nothin'."

Jessie gave me a stern, disapproving look, touched her tan cap and took over the questioning. She didn't like it much if I acted like the boss. Shrugging and smiling inside, I concentrated on my thumbnail again.

"What happened on the train?" Jessie's voice had softened.

I swatted a fly away from my ear.

Helen sniffled and bit down on her lip. "I knew I shouldn't have boarded the minute the train left, but I'd done it. I had this stupid notion that I could get Bev aside and talk to her—convince her that she should divorce him and let him come to me." Hesitating, Helen fidgeted in her chair. "I figured I'd deal with Moon later."

"And?" Jessie said.

"I, uh, saw them in the viewing car. My plan was to win him over. Let him compare me with his wife in plain sight. But when I entered, Simon got up and headed in the opposite direction. Mad, I went over and took his seat. Part of me said to keep quiet, that the whole thing was a waste of time. But, I just couldn't. I pulled out a photo I had of Simon and me together in their bed at their Boston home and stuck it in her face."

"You *didn't*?" I said. "What a hoot!"

Helen straightened her shoulders and gave me the evil eye. "I did! I had every right. He swore he was leaving her. While Bev was staring at us all tangled up together, I confessed everything. About our times in Matlacha, my visit to Boston while she was in Italy—our love for each other."

"How'd she take it? I'd be incensed."

"Oh, she was. Her face got really red—like some damn fire engine or something. I mean, she was mad. When she turned to look at me, I was scared of being that close to her. I swear if she'd had a knife or gun she would have killed me right then."

"Jesus, what did you do?"

"I got out of that car as fast as I could. Then got off at the next station. Took the next train back to Orlando. I tell you, I ain't seen nobody's eyes that looked like that before. Hope I don't ever again. No man is worth being killed for. No man."

Jessie cleared her throat, nodded for me to remember who she was and who I was—me being the sidekick, her being the P.I. Although how many times have I heard her declare she ain't! Like make up your mind, woman! She asked the next question. "Have any idea what time it was that you told her this?"

Helen blinked for a minute or two as if to adjust to the fact that Jessie was still in the room, then said. "All's I know, it happened right after I got on the train."

"Did you see Breece?"

Helen looked puzzled, pursed her lips and shook her head. "Nah. Was he on there?"

Jessie said he was, then asked: "Anything else you can tell us that could help?"

You can bet I registered the fact Jessie said "us" not "me." You can bet.

Helen shrugged and shook her head. Her face darkened. Her lower lip quivered. "I don't seem to be grieving like I should be." She turned back to me—her poker bud. "Does that make me a bad person? Am I shallow?"

I pulled off a loose piece of fingernail and flicked it into the nearby ashtray. "Maybe you didn't love him as much as you reckoned. Maybe it was the thrill of secrecy that tied you two together. Hard to tell. Sometimes we just don't get no answers to things."

Helen's eyes moistened.

Poor kid. I poked her gently on the arm. "Don't worry kiddo. You're still part of our poker group. That's cool, ain't it?"

Helen said nothing, but I could see from the expression in her peepers that she was chewing over the info like a piece of toffee.

Jessie stood. Jotting down her number, she said if Helen thought of anything else she should call.

14

Jessie said she craved a walk, so we trotted under the blue sky like two ponies. As usual, she was moving too fast. I was trying to keep up and getting grumpier with each step.

"Okay, I'm ready. Let's go see this Moon person," Jessie finally said. "See what she has to say."

"Wait `til you meet her. You're going to love her."

"I'll try not to," Jessie said.

I looked at her sharply. "Oh, yeah, right—you need to stay objective—me too. Well, this'll be a test. The woman is like a good beer—refreshin` any time."

"You were a bit ruthless in there earlier at one point," Jessie said. She swung her arms higher, lengthened her stride.

I was beginning to feel like an engine that could (but couldn't) going up a steep incline. Huff. Huff. Crap! I coughed. "Hey, could you slow the pace a stitch. Have mercy! I ain't no athlete like you."

Jessie slowed down. I stopped and leaned forward and breathed deeply in and out for several seconds before walking up to her where she was waiting. "I can't stand it when women think men are better than them. Drives me up the wall."

"Yeah. Yeah. But just watch your mouth. We're partners. What sticks to your back sticks to mine. We don't need to be accused of browbeating people who're in mourning. This is a small village. Besides, if Helen was thinking of revenge, she'd already pushed him off a pedestal. And she *was* on that train. And she *did* follow up with her plan. Who says she didn't poison Simon before she got off? Who says Helen's story is true? Seems like she was doing everything she could at the end to get sympathy, don't you think? You sure were buying her act."

I raised and lowered my eyebrows several times like that old comedian used to do that I watched on Netflix once in a while—Groucho something or other. "Ah, hah, the plot thickens and the P.I.'s on top of things."

Jessie laughed. I winked at her. The truth was—she was the P.I., not me, I had to give her that.

"Come on," Jessie said, "let's see if Moon's home."

Letting Jessie knock, I stood to her right so I could see her face. No way did I want to miss her first glimpse of the legendary Moon McCain.

My heart snickered as the door opened.

Bee-hive pale blonde. False eyelashes. Hooped earrings. Lips the size of elongated plump grapes above a deep dimpled chin. Size 42 girls. Bling-studded short shorts. Long willowy legs that never seemed to end. Four-inch gold lame` heels. Six four or five—no one dared to ask. Like a one hundred and fifty pound glittering mermaid, Moon McCain stirred up

85

the tongues around Matlacha so often, I swore she was a relocated underwater critter come here just for the pleasure of lazy islanders.

My gaze flicked back to Jessie's face. Crap! Jessie's expression never changed. Most couldn't hide their awe on first sight of this former, flamboyant basketball star.

"Ladies," Moon said, looking down at us.

I introduced Jessie and told Moon why we were there: To investigate the death of Simon Hill. When Moon glanced behind her, Jessie nudged me in the ribs, so . . . Crap! I'd talked too much again. I mean, I didn't tell her we were there to accuse her of killing Hill, had I? Good grief!

Moon, seeming amused, ducked her head and stepped back.

A purple yoga mat was spread out in the center of the room that contained four pillows. A large head of a female Buddha was framed by the window casing. Threads of Injun (and I don't mean American Injun) music slithered around me like some lazy ole snake wantin` ta dance. "Way cool!" I said.

Moon nodded. "The key, little-un, is to think less is more."

Ain't that what Jessie's trying to teach me? Super, way, way COOL! Admiring the room, I already saw myself loading my car up with junk from my place for the thrift store.

Jessie asked if Moon minded if *she* (Yeah! Yeah! I heard the pronoun emphasis!) asked some routine questions. Moon was more than happy to oblige.

I took out my sidekick notepad.

"Full name?" Jessie said.

"Moon McCain."

I scribbled.

"No, I mean the name you were given at birth," Jessie said.

"Moon McCain. Mom's name was Spring. Dad's name was Winter. It's the truth." She tossed her head back and shrieked. I nudged Jessie and nodded toward a spot to her left.

Jessie's eyes went wide. "That a rat?" she asked in a hushed whisper.

"Ah, don't worry about Vinnie. He's okay." She snapped her fingers.

The rodent scurried across the floor and climbed up onto Moon's folded legs. Turning, it raised its snout high and I swear it nodded a greeting.

"Vinnie's been with me since he was a babe. Don't worry about him. He's had his shots."

"O . . . kay, right, and you're from?" Jessie asked, not taking her eyes off Vinnie.

"Born and raised in Chicago. Moved here in August. First time living anywhere else."

"And you like it?"

"You bet."

"Occupation?"

"Plumber."

"Hey, I got a leaky drain." I said, "You fix things like that?"

"Sure. What do you think plumbers do? Wash windows?" At that question, Vinnie put his head to the side and looked at me like I had four arms.

I know when I've said something dumber than dumb. I don't need it rubbed in. I pressed my lips together and gave Jessie space to continue, which she seemed relieved to do.

"Where did you meet Simon Hill?"

I saw a slight flinch cross Moon's face, then disappear quicker than that rat dashing across the floor which it just did again. I pulled my legs closer to my bod.

"In Boston. I was visiting an aunt on Memorial Day weekend. Simon, Bev and I saw each other at the parade. I was wearing my orange jumpsuit. They said I looked like a poppy. Liked them right away.

"We spent the afternoon at the Savoy. You ever been at the Savoy? So cool."

"So, it was a tryst?" The words slipped out in a funny whisper-like sound which was quite embarrassing.

"Ah, what a big word for you, my little one—tryst. I like to think of it more as group therapy."

I pouted. "How come everyone else has all the fun? Damn!"

Moon gave me a wide smile.

Jessie rolled her eyes then focused on Moon again. "You don't seem particularly upset about Simon Hill's death."

"Oh, I'm sad enough all right. It's always a shame when a person leaves this life."

"This life?" I said.

Moon chose a pale tan pillow to hug. "Sure. I'm sure he'll come back in another body someday." She looked at Jessie. "Don't *you* believe in reincarnation?"

"Well, guess I do," Jessie said. "I got this notion that my first fella is now a pelican."

"I believe it too," I chimed in. "No doubt in my mind that my second foster care pa is now a disgustin` cockroach."

Moon chuckled, then sobered. "I heard Simon was murdered on a train. Got any suspects?"

"Working on that," Jessie said.

"And I'm a possibility, huh? Well, for your information I had no reason to hate him nor his wife and I certainly was not on that train they took from Boston to Orlando."

"How did you know they stopped in Orlando?" Jessie asked.

Moon shrugged. "Isn't that where the train ends?"

"Where were you on that afternoon?"

"Fixin` the sink at the candy store here in Matlacha. You can ask Chris about that."

"Oh, I will. Got any idea who might have wanted Hill dead?"

"The sheriff asked me that. She and her deputy just left, by the way. I'll tell you the same thing I told them. There is only one person I could point a finger at."

"Yeah?"

"Paul Lowinski."

"The *preacher*? Coconut Paul? Ah, come on!" I exclaimed. Everyone knew how kind he was. Hell, he had once fronted me for a loan.

Moon ran her tongue around her mouth and turned toward Jessie. "I saw an argument between the preacher and Simon in late August. Before I split, Simon had a black eye and his nose looked real funny. Coconut Paul was sprawled out bleedin' on the ground. He didn't look so good either."

"Simon Hill was here last summer?"

"Yep."

"Did you and he . . .?"

"Nope. First time I realized he was in town was when I ran into that fight. I planned to stop in to see Simon that night, once he cooled down. But when I went to his house, the lawn guy said he had flown back to Boston."

"Was Bev with him?"

"Don't know."

"Hm," Jessie said, more to herself than to me or Moon, "wonder if Hill was in a habit of coming to Matlacha in the summer months? And if he wasn't, why last summer?"

Moon raised her hands in a gesture that said she had no idea.

15

Coconut Paul was most likely a little younger than Gator, but not as ruggedly handsome. His thick copper hair was curly and brushed with white wisps. With an egg-shaped head that looked super-sized for his skinny bod and his cigar-colored complexion, it wasn't too hard to see where he got his handle.

"Why, bless your souls. You come right in." He was holding a fishing rod with a broken tip.

Like many guys on the islands, he was bare-chested—a fact which enraged me—see what would happen to me if I ran around without my shirt!! I smiled, remembering Jessie and me naked in a kayak adventure at the end of the season last year. So cool! Like mine, Coconut's cut-off jeans were bait-splattered. His chest and a spot on his forearm looked like he'd just been to the doc and had cancer spots burnt off. A wooden plague over a table was imprinted with the words: "*Ye shall make you no idols nor graven images . . . John 11:25.*"

Something was wrong with his quote, but I let it pass.

The room reeked of fried fish which made my gut gurgle with hunger, and cigarette smoke, which made me clamp my lips together in yearning. Daydreaming about having a cig as I walked, I collided head-on with a closed sliding glass door. "SH . . . IT!"

"God bless you, woman. Are, you okay?" Coconut asked as he and Jessie rushed to my side.

Seeing glistening starfish, I pushed away their hands and assured them I was golden. Like crap I was. I needed a drink. Since when did men have such clean glass! Christ! Didn't this joker know there was a purpose for dust and smudges? I rubbed my head.

Coconut Paul offered me an ice pack but when I refused he slid open the offending door and took us to the back cobblestone patio. Shoving a tackle box and a bible over as we sat, Jessie and he spent a few minutes discussing the weather and wonders of being so lucky as to have found such a slice of paradise on earth while I let my starfish resettle in the sand of my mind. Then: "You sure you don't want an ice pack, little woman?" Coconut asked me. "You're getting quite a goose egg."

"Nah, it's just a small concussion. I get `em all the time."

They both nervously chuckled, then Coconut's expression greyed. He adjusted himself on his chair so that he seemed inches taller and said, "So to cut to the chase, I know why you're here. And to set things straight up front: No *I* did not kill Simon Hill. I don't care what that lowlife (May God forgive her) Moon McCain is saying."

Jessie didn't skip a drum beat. "My, my," she said, smiling at him, "news *does* travel fast on the islands, doesn't it?"

I could just imagine what my redheaded friend was thinking: This jerk's a preacher?

Jessie's eyes flitted to a piece of paper that stuck out from the black bible. It appeared to be a list of names. She leaned forward. "Your congregation?"

I giggled.

Coconut frowned, and swifter than an amber jack after bait leaned forward and withdrew the list. At first, he tried to make light of his action. Privacy issues he said.

Uh, huh.

The water in the canal churned with the arrival of hungrier-than-hungry swarming, flapping fish—a momentary distraction.

Coconut looked from Jessie to me and back to Jessie. "Well . . . if you must know, it's a list of residents who signed our petition to stop the annexation of those six parcels of land on Pine Island Road by the evil City of Cape Coral."

"Go on," Jessie said.

"If you haven't heard, the city of Cape Coral just issued a statement that they have full intention of annexing that property. They refuse to talk to us. Communication channels have been blocked. It's been very frustrating, but I am sure they will see God's ways soon and do right by the residents of Matlacha who want to stay as we are."

"What was Simon Hill's position on all this?"

"Well, I found that out on a day I'm not proud of. I'm afraid I fell to sin on that day. I'm sure that handmaiden told you that she saw Simon and me in a struggle. Well, yes, it was more than a struggle, it was a brawl over good and evil. Simon let down his guard and made the mistake of telling me that he was all for the Cape annexing that land. He said that area has always been an eyesore and the Cape could have it. He, in fact, boasted that he helped with the 2012 purchase. He went on and on about how it would raise our property values.

"I couldn't believe it. Where was his conscience I asked him? Of course I thought of Paul's words in Acts 24:16 and quoted them to him: *"'And herin do I myself, to have always a conscience void of offence toward God and toward men . . .'"* He laughed at me. That's when I sinned. *"'Vengeance is mine, I will repay, says the Lord,'"* I cried out. And let him have it good. Real good—broke his nose I heard. I've prayed for forgiveness since."

Paul actually had tears in his eyes. He really did!

Embarrassed, I tried not to look at him. Good grief, get a grip, man. I glanced at Jessie. She was looking out the window.

"Any Christian knows that passage is about *not* taking revenge, but allowing God's wrath to do it for you. Miss Carolyn, do you think God will ever forgive me?"

I tried to hide my startled (I'm sure), expression. Where did this jerk learn my given name? Who gave him permission to use it? I bit back my angry retort. "Oh, sure. Course he will." I turned to Jessie. "Don't *you* think?"

She cleared her throat. "Absolutely. God er, uh, Jesus forgives. Everyone knows that. Uh, did you tell others about what Hill said?"

"Of course I did. Everyone deserves to know how residents stand. Helps us understand what kind of evil we're up against."

I leaned in close to him. "So, what's your beef with Moon?"

Coconut's face paled then reddened. He stiffened. Dropped his hands between his knees. "That's between Moon and her maker."

"And you?" I said.

Coconut shrugged and rubbed the bible he was still holding.

"Anything to do with Hill or this annexation issue?" Jessie asked.

"Nope. Not a thing."

"Then it's none of our business. Right, Zen, er Miss Carolyn?"

I sent her two eyefuls of switchblades. "Right."

Coconut continued. "Funny. I had this dream the other night. Jesus walked into this cave and commanded that Simon Hill rise from the dead and he did. Odd, huh?"

"Like Lazarus?" Jessie said.

Paul's eyes filled with tears again.

Was he kidding?

"And who so ever liveth and believeth in me shall never die. Believest this?" he said looking earnestly at both of us.

At the same moment (exactly) Jessie and I pushed ourselves out of our chairs, excused ourselves, and power walked around the house. Not that we were in a hurry to leave the guy or nothing. Nothing like that.

"Whew! Where does he preach?" Jessie asked.

"HAH! There's no building no congregation—just folks he runs into or on a street corner. I'm sure he's not ordained or nothin`. Sad, ain't it?"

"He's downright freaky!"

95

I laughed. "You think?" I smacked Jessie. "Don't ever call me Ms. Carolyn again."

Jessie rubbed her forearm. "Won't."

"Just don't ever. Not even in fun."

"Okay. Okay. I won't. *Relax*, Zen!"

16

That night after leaving Zen, I put my iPad on the table under the window facing the pass and typed in "Matlacha Florida Annexation." The first article that popped up had been reported by Fox 4 News and it stated that the protestors were upset about the City of Cape Coral's 4-3 vote to approve the annexation of about 5.4 acres of land along Pine Island Road. Matlacha and Pine Island residents wanted Matlacha to stay the same, not wanting three to five boat ramps added when there was already a boat ramp in place. Fear of increased traffic on land and on the water was listed as a major concern. The estuary and animal and sea life was listed as one as well. The article included a quote by Breece Devino, "We don't want Cape Coral, we don't want Cape Coral zoning, we are Pine Island and we are probably going to leave Lee County and start our own government so we have a voice." Sounded reasonable enough. But his last words were more volatile. "We're sick of being pushed around by the government. We know what we want, but we're not sure what they want. They won't talk to us. We're tired of begging. We're fighting mad."

A second article printed by NBC NEWS in January was about a lawsuit of more than two-hundred pages filed by residents in Matlacha against the City of Cape Coral. The lawsuit challenged the annexation. Paul Lowinski was quoted more than once. Not too surprising, each quote ended with a bible verse. My eye scanned the last paragraph of the article about a disturbance at the last Matlacha meeting. Apparently an unidentified man spoke up in favor of the Cape Coral plans and before he could get his statement fully read he was mobbed and shoved out the door by other residents. Could that man have been Hill? If not, who was he?

Hmm.

I placed some calls.

17

Gator and I were gossiping about Jessie over a beer.

"Yeah, somethings buggin` Jessie, but don't know what."

Gator spit out the last quarter inch of a stick he'd been chewing. "Saw her last night after midnight on the bridge, staring into the water. That ain't right."

"Whoa! Roger that. She's an early to bed gal."

"Yep. Everyone knows that. Stopped to talk to her, but she wasn't having any, so I left her be. Reckon she could use a female friend. Sometimes two women can talk easier like."

"You got that right." I pushed up from my chair.

Gator niggled at a scab on his hand. "Heard you're investigating Hill's murder."

"Yep."

"Reckon if you need help, you'll ask me."

"Reckon so."

"Got any suspects yet?" he asked.

"There's always plenty of suspects."

"Any clues staring you in the face?"

"Other than the fact he was poisoned on a train, we ain't pinpointed any yet. Jessie's waiting to hear what kind of poison was used."

"Poison, huh? I'm thinking that's a woman's way of killing."

"Hey, that's downright sexist!! Plenty of suspects. Men and women. But Hill *was* quite the lady's man, so maybe more women than men. Well, guess I'll go see Jessie."

"Give her a 'Hey' from me."

I nodded and went into my trailer.

Ever since the conversation with Jessie about her need to improve her P.I. skills I'd been wondering what the real reason was for all that change. I should have pried more. Something just might be growing in her innards. Guess I'd see if I could slice her flesh enough for that worm to crawl out.

I grabbed a package of Oreos, my cowboy hat, and my gator hunting vest, pulled on my new red boots and went back outside.

"That gal won't know what hit her," Gator said, winking and standing.

"You're darn tootin' she won't."

18

Jessie was sitting on the inn dock, easel and canvas in front of her. A pelican sat on the furthest piling. A water moccasin slithered its way under the dock. I turned toward Jessie. The set of her shoulders confirmed she'd been there quite some time. The canvas was empty. A charcoal pencil balanced on the arm of her chair.

"Hey, gal! What's up?" I said, lowering myself into the green Adirondack beside her and stretching out my legs.

"Nice boots," she said.

"Yeah! Cost me my tips, but, oh, yeah! They is fine!"

Jessie's smile was so fake it hurt my instep.

I pulled out the bag of cookies from my LV leather (well, it looked liked one, no one would guess) handbag, ripped the bag open and held it toward her. She sighed, said thanks and pulled out two. I took three, set them in my lap and pulled out two bottles of milk. Jessie set her bottle on the plank near her right arm. I opened mine and took a long swallow, then chomped my first cookie in half and chewed. A group of five kayakers paddled past. We waved as they neared but continued to eat and drink.

The pelican raised its wings and soared over the kayaker's heads. Vehicles roared and growled across the nearby drawbridge.

ı

I handed Jessie the bag again. She took one more cookie. I took out four.

"No inspiration?" I asked, wiping a crumb from the corner of my mouth.

Raising the bottle to her lips, she shook her head just once.

"So, hear you've become a night owl."

"You've talked to Gator."

"Here, have another cookie, then tell me what's buggin' you."

"No, thanks, I've had enough." Her lips began to work. The fingers of her left hand tapped the arm of her chair. She straightened. "If you must know, it's the Iranian woman."

"What about her?"

"She reminds me of someone."

"Yeah?"

"Not a pretty story, but, well . . . Here, give me another Oreo."

I did and Jessie began to talk. "When I was sixteen my best friend was from Iran. Lots of kids steered clear of her—said she was too scary— but I liked her. She was real smart and a good person. If it weren't for Bahar I wouldn't have passed math."

I nodded and took another swallow of milk.

"One day we were in the school restroom and two male upper classmen came in."

"In the girl's restroom?"

"Yeah. They backed us into corners, covered our mouths and the guy who had Bahar yanked up her long skirt all the while calling her an

Islamic pig. I managed to knee the guy who had me cornered and got free."

"Did they . . . ?"

"I wasn't raped, but Bahar . . . I . . . I'll never forget her sobs."

"So you must have nailed them good, right?"

Jessie lowered her head. "That's the thing. Bahar begged me to keep quiet about it. She said her parents would disown her if they found out. She would be ruined and never be able to marry."

"So you never turned them in?"

"Never."

"And you stayed in the same school with these guys? How could Bahar ever feel safe?"

"She stopped coming to school."

"Like, forever?"

"Yeah. I don't know what she admitted to her parents, but she never returned to school and I never saw or heard from her again."

"And those guys?"

"Oddly enough, they were killed in a car accident two weeks later. Drunk as skunks. The other car they hit had a mother and two kids in it. The kids were killed."

"Damn!"

"Yeah. If we'd turned those guys in, those kids would never have been killed."

"Christ!"

Jessie squeezed her eyes shut and pushed herself out of her chair, dropping cookie crumbs onto the dock. "I'm concerned I'm not going to be objective where Shirin is concerned. I just don't think I can do it. But I have to think she might have killed Hill. I have to." She began to pace, then stopped in front of me. "Zen I really want Shirin to be innocent. I really want to help prove she is! But, we both know . . . Oh, Zen . . ."

19

"Hand me one of those, will ya?" I said, tilting my red Stetson toward the back of my head.

I was standing next to Gator watching him pull off a half-eaten shrimp from his fish hook. Traffic rumbled across the bridge. I bent down and took out one bigger than my thumb and handed it to him. "How come you just don't cook the shrimp and eat `em? Seems a waste ta use `em as bait."

"There's fishin` and then there's eatin`," he mumbled, hooking the shrimp through its back and flipping the line back into the water.

"When you're done, if you got any left, drop them off at my place. I didn't put out any meat for supper."

"If you're lucky, you'll get better than that. Just hold your horses."

I leaned on the railing and watched his bobber for a spell. Gator was lucky. He loved fishin`. Me? I'd tried it, but it never took. Too much quiet time. Too much . . . well, it just didn't take.

Gator sniffed and tugged at his right earlobe. "So, you talked to her?"

"Yep."

"Anything you feel right tellin` me?"

"Let's just say she's bugged by an incident of her past. You know the kind, the ones that screw us up forever."

"Thought it might be something like that. Hey! Look over there."

I frowned and turned my head. A woman carrying a small manila package climbed out of a white car and hurried into the post office. "Whoa! That's her!" I took off at a dead run. But the ongoing and oncoming traffic didn't let up for me to cross the road. I yelled when Shirin came out. She apparently heard me because she ducked her head, got into the car and managed to drive onto the road before I could cross. Running, I tried to catch up with her, but only was able to bang on the back of her car once before it shot forward out of reach. Shirin was the last car to cross over the bridge before a flashing light signaled the drawbridge was raising. "Damn!"

I pulled my cell phone out of my pants pocket and clicked on Jessie's name. "Come on. Come on. Answer. Jessie! It's Shirin. She's in a white Honda. She just crossed the bridge, if you're at the inn you might be able to way . . ." The phone went dead. I slid it back into my pocket.

Gator stood on the opposite side of the road waving at me with his pole. I stepped down from the walkway and weaved through the cars and trucks that were now waiting for the drawbridge to lower.

"That was close," he said.

"Yeah. Jessie may be able to waylay her on the other side."

"Fat chance."

"But a chance. Did you get the license plate number?"

"I thought you told me she took her cousin's car."

"Oh, yeah." I pushed my Stetson back and wiped sweat off my forehead. "Whatever. You didn't want nothin`?"

Gator grinned and held up a sea bass. "Supper," he said.

"Good god, man, I was in the middle of something important!"

"Seems like you'd already lost her." He spit a wad of tobacco into the water. "You sure you don't need my help?"

Sending him an eye dagger or two, I shook my head, turned and headed in the direction of the inn.

20

"Open the door, Shirin! Please open the car door!" I glanced behind me. Drawbridge still up. Damn!

A scraggly-haired man coming out of Bert's pointed at me as I pounded furiously on the passenger window of the car. The driver in front of Shirin was craning his neck to watch us. I turned my back on him and banged harder. "Open the damn door!"

Click.

I yanked the handle hard, the door popped open and I slid inside.

Shirin refused to look at me. She inched the car forward, then pressing on the brake too fast, the car lurched. She repeated the same move. "Why don't you pull over and I'll drive," I said.

She gripped the steering wheel harder and pushed down on the gas. We shot forward. I put my flip flop on the dashboard. The car stopped about an inch from the car in front of us. "Hey!" In less than a block we would be at her cousin Mahta's home. I invoked all the good Karma I could muster and held my peace.

When she turned onto the gravel parking area, she drove toward the back of the building and parked the car with a jerk in the middle of the lot. Fine by me. I just wanted out.

We left the car and I walked quickly to her. "You scared us by disappearing like that," I said.

She said nothing.

"Let's go inside." I took her arm, more to make sure she didn't run in the opposite direction than to assist her.

I knocked on the door. When Mahta answered she exclaimed and pulled Shirin inside. As they went down the short hallway, they spoke Persian (I only knew this from Bahar telling me what language her mom spoke). Leaving the door ajar, I hesitated and texted Zen. *Got her. Come to Mahta's pronto!*

Seeing Shirin again left me on shaky emotional ground. She could easily be Bahar's mother. And all I felt when I was reminded of Bahar was Guilt with a capitol G and a deep sense of loss. Guilt was one of my worst nemeses. Hadn't the notion that I'd most likely helped cause my first lover's suicide almost eaten me alive? That is, before I proved he was murdered. I stepped back outside and leaned against the wall. The women were sitting now, still talking in loud voices.

Gravel crunched. I almost cried out in joy when Zen ran around the corner.

Realizing I was over-reacting and teetering toward the vulnerable side of the fence, I readjusted my attitude. "What took you so long?" I asked.

She leaned over at the waist, panting. "Next time I buy boots, they're havin' rubber soles. God, my feet will never be the same." She straightened. "She inside?"

I nodded and started in. The Iranian women, like two frightened mallards, were huddled together on the sofa. Zen and I took chairs facing them.

"Have any water?" Zen asked, pulling out her notepad.

Looking at her solid presence, I felt my shoulder muscles relax and crossed my ankles. Concentrated on Shirin.

Mahta excused herself.

"You okay?" I asked.

Shirin shrunk back into the cushions.

Zen touched my arm and leaned forward. "Hey! Woman! Sit up straight. Jessie Murphy is talkin` to ya."

The harsh demand worked. Shirin slid forward on the sofa and put her feet squarely on the floor, hands intertwined in her lap.

Zen's eyes were hard, her tone surly but low. "That's better. Now pay close attention `cause Jessie is real annoyed you took off like that. She has questions for you. Questions you better answer truthfully or, or, well, you just better do it, that's all."

Mahta stepped into the room, carrying a tray of water glasses. Zen and I downed our water in three gulps. Shirin didn't touch hers. Mahta sat the tray on the coffee table and settled close to Shirin.

"Okay, Shirin," I said, "tell us why you left and where you went."

Shirin's eyes remained on the floor. She said nothing.

"NOW!" Zen shouted.

The women looked startled (I'm sure I did too). Mahta wrapped her arm around her cousin's shoulder. "Please. Please. Let me talk to her. "Please!" she pleaded.

Zen and I slid back in our chairs and waited as Mahta spoke to Shirin. When Mahta was finished, Shirin mumbled something and Mahta turned to us. "She'll talk now."

Zen took out her pen.

"Tell us why you left," I repeated.

Her voice was low, but surprisingly steady. I had expected more quiver. Was Shirin stronger than I imagined?

She raised up on the cushion as she spoke, looking me in the eye, ignoring Zen. "I'm a coward," she said. "Plain and simple. I was afraid that when you found out the truth about me, and I knew eventually I would either have to tell you or you'd find out another way, that you would refuse to help find the killer."

"Without knowing the full truth, no one can or will help you," I said.

"I suppose."

"What made you think that just taking off would help?"

"Oh, I admit now, that was foolish. I had a weak moment. Of course I would have to face you sooner or later—that is, if you decided to help me."

"Where did you go?"

"A hotel in Arcadia."

"You *drove* there?"

"Yes. Slowly."

"I should hope so," I said, remembering her earlier driving performance.

"So, what is it you're hiding from us?" Zen asked.

Shirin crossed her legs. "I lied about not knowing what happened to my husband's killer. He was killed several years after the, uh, robbery."

"Okay, and . . ."

"I killed him."

Like drop a bomb in the room! Even Zen looked taken aback.

"I was caught. I was released from prison only recently."

"How did you find him?"

"Like seeing Hill, it was purely accidental. He came into a coffee shop where I worked. At first, I wasn't sure it was him, but he began coming in routinely. After about a month, I knew it was him. A week later he was dead."

"How did you do it?"

"Poison in his coffee."

Oh, shit. Poison. A coincidence? Could I really believe this?

"But, Ms. Murphy, I will say again, I did not kill Simon Hill. With more time, I might have. But that was the first time I saw him and I was unprepared."

Unprepared? Like she didn't have any poison with her? Had there been regret in her voice? Was I in Rod Serlings *Twilight Zone*?

Shirin looked first at Zen and then at me. "I repeat. I did not kill Simon Hill and I need your help to find the killer before I am arrested for doing it. After all, I have a sound motive. Simon Hill raped me that night

112

while my husband watched, just before the other man, while laughing, shot my husband."

21

Bahar was the smart one. I, the creative one. We'd known each other since we were twelve. Shared our pride when we had our periods and became women. She was joyful, hopeful, brimming with plans for the future. Her favorite class was science. Mine was art. She loved strawberries on ice cream, I preferred bananas. Her? Pepperoni pizza. Me? Mushroom and onion. Her skin was like satin. Mine was dotted with freckles. She preferred purple nail polish to my red. Unbuttered popcorn to my extra-buttery.

We were BFFs for four years before we walked into that school bathroom. She never returned to school. Refused my calls. My texts. Didn't answer the door when I knocked.

By keeping our secret, by blocking out the full truth from even myself, I'd lost my best friend and two kids were killed.

Months later I learned the family had moved back to Iran. When we were thirteen, Bahar professed why she would never want to return to her country. Except while in their home, she would have to be fully covered in black. Her cousin, at sixteen, had already spent several days in prison. Once for being turned in when a man saw the bottom of her jeans below her chador. Once for wearing pink nail polish.

"Jessie to earth. Jessie to earth," Zen said.

I leaned back on the yellow Adirondack chair and looked at her, smiling thinly. "Sorry, what were you saying?"

"I was saying that it's really, really hard to believe Shirin would kill her husband's murderer and not the one who raped her and watched her husband be executed. Don't you agree?"

"Sure. Of course," I mumbled.

"That woman is no weeping wallflower," Zen said, "She's gutsy as hell."

"Yeah, I noticed."

"Plus, when she got out of her car and headed for the post office she was carrying a package. She must have mailed it. I want to know what was in that package."

"So you think we should continue to investigate? I was sure you'd think we should drop the case. Hill being so evil and all."

"I admit, I thought of that, but as you said, we have Shirin to think about. Although her story is too pat and I can't figure out why, I don't think she killed Hill. I think she would have once she had time to buy some poison, but, well, I think she didn't get the chance."

"Not exactly a great client to have," I said.

"Hah! But quite a challenge, right?"

22

After Zen left I took my sketchpad and pencil out and began to draw while Gar watched. It still made me feel content to have my plaster of Paris yard art friend close by. Maybe Will, my first lover, had been right; I had just a tad too much superstitious Irish blood in me. Gar was my good luck charm, my bud. An object that I would grab first if my home ever caught fire. So shoot me.

Soon I had a mug shot of Moon McCain and Coconut Paul to add to my collection.

I withdrew my cellphone from my pocket and asked Siri for the number of the Orlando police department. Tapping on the number, I requested to be put through to the person in charge of the Simon Hill homicide. I introduced myself and declared my role in the case.

"This is an active investigation. We don't share info with P.I.s," he said.

"No chance?" I asked.

"Not a chance. Besides, you're in Matlacha you say?"

"Yes."

"Well, this is Orange County, not Lee. If we feel we need to send detectives down there, we'll do it. Yeah, be right with you. Hey, sorry to be so abrupt but got to go. Bye now."

I hadn't expected anything different. Cops didn't think much of P.I.s. But I found out what I wanted—the investigation was still active. Shirin was safe for the time being.

My monkey ringtone went off. Stretching out on the bed, I clicked "Accept."

"Hey! It's Zen. Moon just called. Bev Hill will be here tomorrow morning from Boston."

"So soon? My, my. I'll give her a call and ask to see her ASAP. You in on this?"

"Of course. Just make it after 4:00. And drop by and fetch me. I want to ride in those new wheels of yours."

"Hah! New is a relative term. Wait until you see the rust! And the driver seat rocks back and forth. Besides, we'll walk to her home. Exercise is a good thing."

Zen groaned. I smiled.

"Just give me a jingle when you know the time."

Next I called my former boss, Hawk, and asked him pretty please to find me anything he could on Beverly and Simon Hill and the rest of the suspect list. He reminded me he wasn't a miracle worker and that I should do my own searching on the net. I assured him that he way underestimated himself, but promised him I would, of course, begin doing my own search too. He growled at me in his usual way, causing me to chuckle and to think of my comfort food, Oreos.

Leaving Gar to mind the store, I drove my Honda into Cape Coral and purchased a 5 x 10 inch magnetic sign with no lettering. The woman

117

behind the desk who took my money asked why I didn't want to advertise on it. I convinced her I was using it as a gag joke and would paint a caricature on it.

Taking it outside, I eyed the offending rust spot, hunkered down and slapped on the oversized bandage. Voila`! Ugliness gone. Just like protecting a raw sore. Now, tell me I'm not creative! Grandma Murphy would be proud. Next I drove to a nearby dollar store and bought several plastic toys: a flute, a tambourine, a whistle. Dropping them into my car door pocket, I flexed my muscles. Humming, I reached forward to insert the key in the ignition. Rocking seat? Oh, yeah! Pulling up the floor mat, I gazed down at the parking lot. Great. Just great. Gingerly feeling the ragged edges of the rusted out hole, I surmised it would last for some time yet. Jiving, I started my just named Alice (of Alice in Wonderland fame who didn't have enough sense but to fall into a hole) and revved the motor. Purred like a kitten on steroids.

Oh, yeah. Life was good.

I crossed Pine Island Road on foot at exactly 4 p.m. Zen was wiping her hands when I strolled up to the window of The Olde Fish House. A couple of guys in caps, white muscle shirts and jeans sat at one picnic table. Behind them a pelican raised and lowered its wings on a piling. Zen walked through the door looking more than tired.

"Busy day?" I asked.

"The usual," she said, adjusting her Stetson firmly on her head and hitching up her cut-off jeans.

"You wear boots to work in? Aren't they hot?"

"Nah, just changed into them. Can't get enough of `em." She stepped back into the kitchen. "See you tomorrow, Mack!" She ran her fingers across her hat brim. "So, we're on for the Hill woman. Can't wait to meet her. Where's your car?"

"I said we'd walk. Remember? Walking is good for us."

Zen grumbled some choice words I refused to hear, then said, "Well, just so you know, I've been on my feet all day. I ain't doin` no fast walkin`."

"I get that. But, let's not stop to chit chat with anyone, we're expected in fifteen minutes."

"Heaven forbid," Zen muttered.

"And I didn't tell Bev that we're investigating her husband's murder, so let's tread lightly there. I'm betting that no one passed on that information. As far as she knows, we're coming to give her hugs."

"Roger that."

Bev opened the door on my first knock.

She and I shook hands. "Great to see you again," she said. I covered her hand with my other one.

Then, in a lightening move, Zen stepped around me and as Bev stepped back, she swallowed her in a huge and I mean HUGE bear hug! Bev's face registered surprise, then alarm.

"I am sooo sorry for your loss, you poor dear! Sooo sorry," Zen cooed as she squeezed harder and I was afraid Bev would pop like an over-inflated balloon as Zen gushed on. "Things like this just ain't right! Why,

119

my pet iguana was killed by a crazy neighbor once. It just ain't easy to get over the loss of our loved ones."

Bev, managing to free herself from Zen's bear grip, stepped back and let us enter, although I noticed she stayed several feet away from my sidekick and averted her eyes from her face. I had the urge to give Zen a smack, but restrained myself. I mean, REALLY! Since when did Zen have a pet iguana?

"Excuse the mess," Bev said. "I've just arrived and these boxes came yesterday."

Boxes were stacked everywhere—on the floors, the dining room table, the kitchen countertop.

Bev collapsed on the white leather sofa. "I've had my personal belongings shipped here." She broke into a grin. "It's lovely to know they are here with me."

Everything in the home was high tech modern—chrome and glass. Very pricey.

"I have a consignment company and a painter coming tomorrow to give me estimates on getting rid of all Simon's stuff and painting the walls."

"Ya don't mean the furniture, right?" Zen asked.

"Oh, yes. This is all Simon's taste. It was never mine. I'm looking forward to unpacking my boxes and decorating in my own style. That's why I've had my personal things shipped down.

"When we moved here and bought this house, Simon insisted upon hiring a decorator and he worked with her exclusively. He thought my tastes far too conventional."

I couldn't help but think that Bev was moving pretty fast in making the changes. So much for a respectful mourning period.

"Anyway, ladies. So nice of you to visit me. Ms. Murphy, I will never forget your kindness at the hospital. You were more than thoughtful."

The plan was to let Bev talk. When Bev offered coffee or tea, Zen and I both accepted coffee and she walked to the kitchen. Zen and I remained in the crowded living room.

"Dang, I'd like to have that sofa," she said in a low voice.

"It's bigger than your whole trailer," I said.

"Yeah, I know, but it would look great in front of my fire pot."

"Start saving your money and maybe in a year or two you could afford a cushion."

Zen tossed me a dirty look and slid her Stetson back on her head.

Dishes rattled.

We headed for the kitchen.

Bev had opened a small box that sat on the granite countertop. She held up a mug. "Isn't this the cutest thing?" she asked.

Zen took the mug from her and read: "*I Love my Grandma*. Ah, now that is sweet. So, you have grandchildren?"

Bev's eyes sparkled. "One. A granddaughter. She's my daughter's. Simon was not my daughter's father, by the way. In fact, she and he never got along." She looked at another mug she'd unpacked. "He was absolutely adamant that I not use these. I got so tired of him degrading them that I packed them away. He was relentless in his scorn for them."

Six sleek mugs hung from a rack on a pedestal at one end of the counter. I looked from them to the pink mug with flowers on the brim in Bev's hand. Yes, opposite ends of the decorator spectrum.

Bev held up another cup. "This one says: *Mom's Rock*. I think of this as a perfect cup." Bev shot a look to the contemporary mugs. "I can't wait to get rid of those things. I'm sure the consignment store manager will love them." She handed us each a mug. "Coffee's ready."

After filling them and doctoring them up with half and half and sugar, Bev raised hers. "To freedom," she said.

"To freedom," we repeated.

A woman wouldn't kill her husband because he didn't like her taste, would she? If I believed that, how could I believe the morning news story that a man had killed his wife on a cruise because she wouldn't stop laughing at him? But it was a true. He had. And the sad truth was, Bev could. Besides, she also had seen the pics of Helen and him in their bed. Eww. But, then, what about Moon's story? Something didn't jive.

We settled in the living room.

Zen took off her Stetson and set it on the floor at her feet. Her eyes were on the sofa. She raised her mug, looked directly at Bev and said, "Sounds like your hubby (May he rest in peace) was a controllin' guy."

I choked on my coffee. What a terrible thing to say. How very rude! I mean, he was hardly in his grave and this was his poor widow. But then, the grieving wife had just made a toast to freedom.

And sure enough, Bev didn't seem startled by the statement. Instead, she replied in a distant voice, "Oh, Simon. Poor Simon. You had to feel sorry for him, at least I did. He had so many walls in his world that kept him constricted. He was so concerned about what others thought. I still can't believe he's dead. In fact, this morning when I awakened, I swore he was lying beside me with his arm around me."

"It has to be hard," I said.

"Yes. Yes, it was. The pressure. The steady pressure. His squeeze—so constant."

Bev turned and faced the sliding glass door. Zen and I gave each other a look that transmitted to each other that Bev had confirmed just how controlling the guy was.

"That's another thing to get rid of," Bev said, nodding toward the door.

A yacht that had to be sixty-foot if it were an inch rested on a covered lift on the canal.

"Excessive, don't you think? Simon loved big things." She glanced at me. "But who needs such a large footprint on this earth? It was something we used to argue about quite often. That is, before I stopped arguing. It just wasn't worth it. Nothing I said meant anything to him."

"He was a fisherman?" Zen asked.

"Oh no. He just liked cruising. Eating up tons of fuel. Ignoring how many manatees the propeller harmed along the way. I was only on board once. Once was enough." She set down her mug. "Oh, my. How terrible of me. I'm afraid I'm making it sound like Simon was a bad man. That

123

just isn't true. He wasn't. Not at all. We just had our differences." She smiled a thin smile. "One thing we agreed on was that we should be charitable. We have so much. We agreed we needed to share our good fortune. Simon was on the board of several charitable organizations." She blinked. "It's so important to give back, don't you think?"

In unison, Zen and I nodded.

I was beginning to feel sorry for Bev. What would it be like to live with a controlling person? I couldn't imagine.

Zen gazed at me long enough to make me fidget, then leaned closer to Bev, making Bev slide backward into her cushion. "Hey! I just remembered something!" Zen said, making me cringe in concern of what she might say next.

"Yes, what?" Bev said cautiously before I could stop Zen.

"Rumor has it that you're a good friend with our local lady plumber, Moon McCain. Is that a charitable act or is it the real deal?"

Bev's face reddened. Her fingers clasped and unclasped. It was obvious she was struggling to regain her calm.

Zen inched closer. "Cause if you really are a friend, I could use a favor. I got a leaky faucet and Moon says she's too busy to come fix it. If you could ask her to find some time, well, I'd be real grateful. My water bill is goin' through the roof."

I was like totally beyond amazed. Where did Zen get these notions? Good grief!

Bev had found her equilibrium. She gazed steadily at Zen. "I'm sorry, my dear, but you're misinformed. I know Ms. McCain only in passing. I'm afraid I have no influence with her."

Zen's lips bent downward. "Drat! I'm always gettin` things wrong. Moon said you, your hubby and her were a tryst."

"Zen!" I exclaimed.

Zen reached down to her hat. "Well she did! A tryst, that was what she said, well, at least suggested." As if to make her point more poignant, she plunked the Stetson on her head and grinned.

Bev's face was so red I feared she would explode. When she finally spoke, her voice was chilly, her eyes were cold. "I'm afraid I feel ill. I'm exhausted from the trip and battling with all the details. Do you mind leaving now?" She stood.

"Listen, I am so sorry," I said as we followed her to the door. I felt a bit ill myself. Zen, at times, had no boundaries, no common sense. What was her purpose in insulting Bev Hill? And what made her think we should share what others in our investigation told us?

Zen began talking a mile a second. "Now, hon, I didn't mean that as an insult. In fact, I said to Moon I'd like to be part of a tryst myself." She turned to me. "Didn't I say that, Jessie?"

I put my hands up to ward off any further comment from my loose-lipped, out of control, sidekick. "Zen, I do believe you've said enough. Beverly, please accept our apologies. Zen just isn't herself today. She had a hard day at work. I'm sure she didn't mean anything rude with her comments."

125

The door shut with a resounding click.

I spun around and raising my arms, began power walking away.

Zen ran to catch up to me. "Hey, wait up!"

"What the hell was that all about? Why did you insult her? Good grief, she'll never want to talk to either of us again. What were you thinking?"

"Well, we learned a lot, don't you think?"

"Yeah, we learned that you're totally out of control and that from now on you will not speak at all during an interview. As in—EVER!"

"Hah! You were startin` to feel sorry for her, weren't you?"

I missed a step.

"Now, be honest. You were. Right?"

Dang. I was.

"I saw that look in your eyes. You were ready to believe anything she said."

Dang. I was. Old habits are hard to break. Dang.

"Well, what we learned is that she lied about having a threesome with Moon. And if she lied about that, then she just might be lying about everything. Ain't that possible?"

I stopped and faced Zen. "It is—possible. That is, if they had one," I admitted. "And thank you for seeing what was happening to me."

Zen ran her fingers along the brim of her hat and raising her chin, began to walk. The heels of her boots punished the pavement.

Feeling sheepish, I met her pace. Zen had been a good friend. She'd seen what was happening—that I was feeling sorry for Bev and thus taking her off the suspect list. She remembered I'd asked her to not let it happen, and had figured out a way to change the course of things.

"Well?" Zen said.

"Yeah?"

"Where's my apology?"

"Oh, well, of course. Sorry, kid."

"Sorry, kid WHAT?"

"For stopping me from falling into that "sympathy" place. I guess," I added, "that's why we need each other."

"You're damn right we do. And don't you forget it." Reaching over, she pulled me to her in one of her grizzly bear hugs, almost knocking me off my feet.

23

Later that evening I decided to take my sketchpad to Bowman's Beach on Sanibel. Every once in a while I didn't mind paying the eight bucks plus parking it cost for the venture. Watching the sunset from a beach blanket was a definite soul surge. I admitted to feeling disappointed in myself. Why could I not have noticed what was happening to me as Bev related her sad story? But the fact was, that I hadn't. I should feel proud of myself that I'd had the foresight to ask Zen to help me guard against that weakness, but I didn't. I felt, rather, like a failure. So, having my soul recharged was definitely something I needed.

Sinking my toes into the sand, lifting my face to the sea breeze, smelling the salt air, watching dolphins frolic offshore and pelicans soar across the surface of the water were all lubricating ointment to my soul, my mind and my imagination.

Snapping my red, blue and yellow towel, I spread it on the ground, shoved the pole of my umbrella as deep into the sand as I could and prepared to settle into my temporary beach home. Unbuttoning my shirt, I slipped it off, dropped it near my bag and stepped out of my shorts. I'd purchased my bikini online. Grandma Murphy would be appalled at its skimpiness. But what she didn't see didn't hurt her. And there was no way she was going to see me in this thing. Like, NEVER!

I adjusted my sunglasses, pulled on the straw hat I'd found at Goodwill on the Cape and began applying a generous portion of sunscreen.

Britney Spears` voice and mournful music drifted my way. I smiled, sat and began to doodle. Soon I closed my eyes and inhaled and exhaled deeply.

Laughter. Clapping. More laughter.

"Toss it here!"

I opened my eyes.

Two young women in bikinis with less fabric wasted than my own were playing Frisbee near the water's edge. Tugging on the brim of my hat, I raised myself on my arms in order to see them better. The Frisbee skidded across the sand only feet away. The girl with her back to me swiveled around and ran toward it. After getting a good look at her face, I flipped over so my back was toward the sun and faced her, but kept as hidden as possible under my hat. The Frisbee was in sight. The girl bent low and retrieved it, spun around and tossed it to her companion.

Giving her plenty of time to reach the water's edge, I flipped over again and continued to watch their play, keeping my eyes on them as they jogged to their beach towels, flopped down on their bellies and laid their heads on their arms.

It occurred to me that I should go over and say hello, but then thought better of it. Maybe that would embarrass them? Amish young women were not in the habit of being seen in bikinis. But Amish youth were encourage to take a trip into the outside world before settling into their

129

communities. This must be their opportunity. Why invade their privacy just because we had shared a few words on a train and just because I had loaned them my phone?

Adjusting my umbrella so I had my own privacy, I sat up and began drawing their faces, wondering if they knew how beautiful they were.

Time passed as it should—at the pace of a mother mallard and her chicks crossing a canal. I turned the page. The girls must have fallen asleep. Their music had switched off. I leaned back on my elbows and watched two dolphin rise and disappear. Ah, such peace.

The earth rumbled. Footsteps. Curious, I raised my hat brim and almost let out a "Hey!" but managed to swallow it.

Breece Devino with hair reaching for the sky in a black speedo was hunkered down at the girl's towel. Scooping up two handfuls of sand, he proceeded to let it dribble over their backs. They screamed, jumped up and a sand fight broke out. I wasn't sure what to do. Join them? Stay incognito? Before an answer formed, they grabbed up their towels and their bags and all ran toward the path leading to the lagoon, the beach house and I assumed, the parking lot.

So, what did we have here?

One of our suspects was very friendly with two other people who were on that train. So what if they were Amish? This was odd and definitely worth checking into. How could I find out the names of those young women?

Back at the inn, I sat on a chair near the window. Gar was on the table facing me. It was poker night for Zen so I couldn't call her. I looked at Gar. "So, what do you think?" I asked, after telling him what happened at the beach.

"Did this odd beach meeting tell me anything? Hmm. Well, one thing, those girls were awfully comfortable with Breece. They didn't seem shy in those bikinis."

I rubbed Gar's belly. "Two, Breece was definitely comfortable with both of them.

"I need to know if there is anyway these three knew each other before getting on that train. And just exactly what is their relationship."

I patted Gar's head. "Why, you ask? Because, well, the murder could have been planned by more than one person, depending on the motive. All three were on the train." I touched Gar's wing. "What? You think that's farfetched?" I put the tip of my nose on the tip of his. "It may be, bud, but well, it just may not be too."

Pulling out my phone, I tapped Hawk's number on my "recent" list. He wasn't happy that I added two more nameless people to his list.

24

"Zen, I'm trying to be honest here."

"Honest? Hell, you haven't been honest since the day we met. I call and tell you I can't play poker tonight because I have to fill a shift for someone at work, come home and find you in my trailer rifling through my stuff, a wad of MY money making your shirt pocket bulge. Honest, you say? Get real!"

Breece, with bloodshot eyes, raised his hands and backed away. "Okay, if you don't want to hear me out, that's fine." He reached for the doorknob. "I'm out of here."

"Don't you dare leave! You can't come in here and try to steal my savings and think you can just walk away! Get back over here."

Breece let his arm drop. His head lowered. His voice was low, deadpan. "I would have returned it."

"Sure you would of."

"No, I mean it."

I slammed my hand on the table. "So what did you plan to do with it? Buy more pot and beer?"

"Nah, nah....I have these friends, well they're more than friends, they're sisters and they're in trouble. If they don't pay off a debt by this Friday, well, they'll be roadkill."

"Sisters? Oh, sure, sisters! I should have known—women in trouble and you're being freakin` Robinhood to the rescue. Well, I'm not some rich lord to steal from. Damn, man. I work hard for my money."

"Ah, come on, Zen. I know you do. Don't be mad. I really would have returned it. I don't get paid til the end of the month. You've been in a tight fix before."

"There's something else. What do you do with all those oleander's you're growing in those bean cans? Nobody grows oleander in bean cans."

Breece's eyebrows rose. He sniffed and rubbed his nose. "The oleander? Why ask about that? You ain't thinkin` I made tea out of it, are you? It's all over town that Hill was killed by oleander tea."

My mouth worked. My eyes shot bullets.

"Ah, come on Zen. I ain't no killer. Those are hybrid oleander. I'm growing them from seed for a feller in Arcadia. Shit! You mean all this time you're thinkin` I might of killed Hill? Christ. He wasn't worth my time of day. I sure wouldn't risk getting life in prison for that dirt bag."

I sniffed. "Yeah, right. What's the buyer's name?"

"Richard Rancine."

"Spell that last name." I jotted it down. "Okay, so fool, why didn't you ask for a loan? Why steal it? And ya better have a good answer."

"I should of—I know that now—but, well, I guess I was too damn embarrassed. I mean a guy asking money from a gal. It just ain't right."

"But it's right to steal from a gal? What? Are you nuts?"

"Hey, listen. I knew you were saving for that TV. I figured you wouldn't have enough money `til the end of the month. I take it. Return it. You don't notice. No skin off anyone's nose." His spiked, greased yellow hair looked like he hadn't combed it in a week.

I let out a prolonged gust of air and shook my head, tossing the roll of fifties at his feet. "Go on. Give it to your chicks in need. And get the hell out of here before I call the cops."

He hesitated before scooping it up. Then turned before letting go of the screen door. "I'll repay you at the end of the month."

"You're damn right you will."

The chrome chair almost broke when I collapsed on it. This was news I would not share with Jessie. If she knew Breece was a thief, she'd definitely put him higher on the suspect list. Sisters! Like I believed that! I sniffled. Men could be such jerks. I looked at the piece of paper with Rancine's name printed in red ink. I *would* give that to Jessie. She could find out his phone number easier than I could.

Feeling the fat on my belly with one hand, popping off the lid of a beer with the other, I gazed into a mirror, pulled out my phone and called her.

Maybe tomorrow I'd switch to light beer.

I sucked in my gut.

25

The door to my room at the inn swung wide as Zen entered.

"Ohmigod!" I burst out laughing. "What in the world did you do to yourself? Good god, you look like you can't breathe! What the hell are you wearing?"

Zen headed for the bathroom. Her face was as red as a rooster comb. Her usually prominent belly was like major, no, beyond major—FLAT. Although it took a huge effort, I had stopped laughing, but looking at her, out it came again. She hesitated at the end of the bed and looked over her shoulder. Her words escaped in painful syllables. "Give me a sec. I need to take this damn thing off." And she disappeared into the bathroom.

After wiping the tears from my eyes, I heard an exaggerated sigh and a second later Zen, swinging a body-colored corset like a flag, asked, "Got any beer?"

I burst out laughing again. "You're kidding, right? Do you really think that's wise?"

"Why isn't it? I ain't the only gal in this community wearing fancy undergarments, I can tell you that."

"Oh, I'm sure you're not—not by a long shot. But if you cut down on the beer . . ." I chuckled. Zen glared. I made myself go sober. "Besides, I'm not quite on my game after a drink."

"Well, *I* am."

"Hah! So you say. But wrong o! Alcohol effects your logic."

"Logic? What logic? No one has ever accused me of havin` any of that!"

I rolled my eyes. "Hey, girl. Let's get serious. Got your notebook?"

She withdrew it from her pocket and held it up.

"Good. Let's start with our suspect/motive list, etc. You can chime in whenever you have anything to add," I said.

"Roger."

"According to Hawk, most murders are committed by a loved one, I'll start with Beverly Hill. According to information that Hawk uncovered, Bev indeed is from a wealthy family—an only child. Her father was a real estate giant. When he and his wife died in an airplane crash, she inherited the fortune estimated to be over twenty mil. Before marrying Simon Hill, she was divorced for several years from a golf pro, Forest Johnson. This is the father of her only child—Diane—not married."

Zen raised her notebook and interrupted. "My notes say the daughter and Simon were on the outs. Got any info about that?"

"Actually I do. Hawk discovered that Diane is a lesbian who came out of the closest when she was about twenty. Shortly after, she published an article in her college newspaper about her struggles. Apparently the article embarrassed Simon and he broke off all contact with her."

"Bev said she had a granddaughter."

"She does, but not by blood. Diane and her first partner adopted her. When Diane and her partner broke up, Diane was awarded custody of the child. This next part is quite interesting. As we both know, according to Bev, Simon apparently controlled many aspects of her life. However, what we didn't know is that about a month ago she filed for divorce."

"And Simon knew this?"

"Most likely. Papers are usually served right away."

"And they were still traveling together to Florida, sleeping in the same cabin? How did he convince her to do that? Or vice versa." Zen said.

"Great question. One we need to ask Bev on our next interview—if she will grant us one. After that last fiasco, I have my doubts."

"Yeah. Sorry about that. Don't worry. You get the interview and I'll behave myself."

"Right. Anyway, the only other information I have on Bev is that she married Simon when she was thirty-five and she's fifty-six now."

"Twenty-one years is a long time to be controlled," Zen said.

"One day is too long," I added.

"Roger."

"I'd list her motive as a controlling relationship, jealousy or pure anger at her husband's sexual habits. You got any other idea?"

"Only trouble is, she filed for a divorce."

"Yeah. But also, per the coroner's report that Hawk managed to get, Simon was gradually poisoned over several weeks. Bev would be the natural suspect. She lived with him. Filing for the divorce could have created a smoke screen."

"According to Helen's story and what we got a glimpse of at our interview, that rich gal hides a hot temper."

"Yeah, and there's that."

Zen frowned and asked, "Did the cops find the source of the Oleander tea that poisoned him?"

"I was getting there. I called the investigating detective and twisted his arm for info. Apparently a jar of tea was in Hill's briefcase, half empty with no label. Someone must have given it to him or Bev—someone Hill trusted."

"The cops tell you who their No. 1 suspect is?"

"Hah! Not a chance. But Shirin is still safe from arrest. All's golden there—so far."

Zen was writing in her notebook. She looked up. "Any other questions to ask Bev when we see her?"

"We need to ask her," I gave Zen a warning look. "with more finesse this time, about the supposed sexual experience she and Simon had with Moon McCain. I'd like to know if Hill had so much control of her that he could make her have sex with another woman while he watched."

"Yeah. `cause if that's the case, she must have been a time bomb ready to explode."

"That's my way of thinking too. But then again, she may like such relationships. I've heard of stranger things."

Zen's eyes rounded. "You have? Like what?"

I shook my head.

Zen looked all little-girl innocent. "Uh, huh, sure, that's what I thought." Her eyes began to twinkle. "Now, me? I could fill your ear for some time."

I raised my hand to stop her. "That's okay, Zen. I'm sure you could, but let's stay on track."

"Maybe some night around the fire pot." Her eyes were stars. "Believe me, I got stories."

I cleared my throat and nodded toward her notebook. "Also add that we need to get her talking about her daughter."

"You think the daughter could have killed him?"

"If she witnessed the way Hill treated her Mom, sure."

Zen's pencil moved swiftly across the page. She hesitated and looked up. "Is that it?"

"Not quite. Hawk had some fascinating info about our vic. Hill turns out to be even more of a liar than Breece knew. Not only was he part of the Cape Coral purchase of those parcels in 2012, but he also was CEO of a corporation in line to bid on a high rise on the property if the Cape Coral Council offered it. Jerk."

"IF it goes through."

"Right."

"That creep. He had us all believing he was against the annexation."

"Seems he knew how to manipulate big time, not only his wife—if that is true," I said.

"Do you think Bev knew about this?"

"That's another thing we need to discuss with her. I'd also like to know what she knows about the falling out Hill had with his brother."

Zen wrote furiously.

"Add that Hill was handy, liked cruising on his yacht, hated anything conventional and liked to dance."

She gave me a look that asked: Dancing?

"You never know," I said, shrugging.

"Okay, let's switch to Shirin. She lied to us too. And we don't know yet what was in that package she mailed."

"Correctomundo."

"Okay, now—Breece."

Zen wrote, then looked toward Gar. "So what juicy stuff did you learn about him that I don't know?" Her words were filled with barely-hid emotion.

"Now who isn't being objective?"

Zen lowered her eyelids. "Point taken. Go on."

"Well, what we know is that he was infuriated with Hill over the annexation issue. We both know that he is growing oleander in pork and bean cans . . ."

"So what? Anyone can get oleander leaves by walking into most any yard."

"Zen, I'm just listing what we know. Okay?"

"Hey, listen, I almost forgot." She reached in her pocket and pulled out a piece of paper. "This is who Breece is growing his hybrid oleander for, a guy who lives in Arcadia—Richard Rancine. We might want to contact him."

I took the paper. "So, you're seeing Breece?"

Zen touched her snake tat, then her neck. "We ran into each other–nothing more—and the oleander thing came up." She sniffed and waved the pencil at me to continue.

"Okay, so we also know he was on the train. We know he lied about not knowing Bev and Simon well as the neighbor said she saw him go from the house more than once. And I do believe she said sometimes when only Bev was home. Correct?"

"Yeah."

"That brings me to a very odd thing that happened . . ." I hesitated, then continued. "Last night I went to Bowman's Beach on Sanibel and I saw Breece there with two of the other train passengers. Two young women who I didn't even know were in the area."

"Two, you say?" Zen said.

"Yeah."

"Well, I might be able to add some light to that. Breece swore late last night that his sisters were visiting him."

"Sisters?"

"That's what he said." She narrowed her eyes at me. "Are you telling me they weren't acting like siblings?"

"Well, not exactly that. They didn't do anything that seemed like anything else. It's just that—you don't think Breece is Amish do you?"

Zen laughed. "Who are you kiddin'? Breece—Amish?" She started to laugh again, then didn't. "Were the two woman Amish?"

"When I saw them on the train they were dressed like Amish women. I had no reason to think they weren't. But on the beach they were dressed in skimpy bikinis."

"Strange."

"I assumed they were just feeling their oats. They have every right to do that. But, either Breece is Amish, the young women were in disguise on the train, or they're Amish and not his sisters."

Zen started to open her mouth, clamped it shut, and then said, "I'd like to know which is true."

"Me too. But let's talk to him together. I want to hear every word he uses to explain who they are and who he is."

Neither I nor Zen had any additional information about Moon McCain or Coconut Paul so we spent little time talking about them. After agreeing I'd call Zen tomorrow once I made our first appointment, Zen rushed away. It was Saturday. Zen didn't have to work on Sunday.

Retrieving Gar from the mattress where he'd toppled over after Zen got up, I set him on the table. "Liars. Liars. Pants on Fire," I said as I petted his wing. I pressed my nose against his, then leaned backward. "Odd, don't you think that everyone we've interviewed lied? As in– EVERYONE! Even Zen."

I gazed out the window at the sea. It was peaceful, gentle. A bird swooped the water's surface. I chewed my lower lip, thinking. "And just exactly what is the draw of Arcadia? Why does that name keep coming up?"

26

We saw Bev the next morning after her tennis game. She wasn't happy that I said I wanted to bring Zen, but after I assured her that Zen would remain silent, she gave in. We met at the local coffee shop—a place she said she loved and Simon hated—The Perfect Cup.

Bev's hair was pulled back into a ponytail. The skin on her face flawless. A mole not bigger than a pencil eraser grew near her left nostril. She wore a white form-fitting sleeveless shirt. Her nails were manicured. She sipped on a glass of juice as I sat while Zen went to the back to fill two coffee mugs.

"So, my neighbor informed me that you're investigating Simon's death. Rather odd you didn't bother to tell me that, don't you think?"

"We had actually come to give my condolences, so it didn't seem important at the time."

Bev gave me a sharp look, then eyed Zen's back. "Okay. But who hired you? It seems I would be the one to do that and we both know I didn't."

I crinkled my nose. "I'm sorry. I can't reveal that information. Let's just say it's someone who is as interested as you are in finding your husband's murderer."

"I have full faith in the police. Apparently your client does not."

"Apparently."

Zen, red Stetson pushed back on her head, belly roll draping over the top of her short-shorts, red cowgirl boots sparkling, appeared at the table with two mugs. Bev refused to look at her. Zen grinned, sat, put my mug in front of me and half-turned so Bev could only see her profile.

Bev leaned her head to the right as she looked at me. "I assume you have questions for me? The police certainly did."

"If you don't mind?"

Bev shrugged.

Zen pulled her notebook out of her pocket and opening it, slid it in front of me. I reviewed the questions, nodded and set it down.

"I assume the police asked about how Simon came about having poisoned tea in his possession. Could you tell us as well?"

"Sure. Why not? About six months ago it arrived in our mailbox. There was a gift card that said only one word "Enjoy." No signature. No return address. Whoever sent it must have known Simon was a tea drinker. He began using it about two months ago. He said it was delicious."

"And you never had any yourself?"

"No, I'm a coffee drinker. That was one thing Simon didn't try to change about me."

"And when did his stomach problems start?"

"Not long after. But they were mild at first, just an annoyance."

"Did anyone see the package?"

"My daughter was there when Simon opened it."

"You said your daughter and Simon didn't get along?"

Bev turned the gold band on her left finger. "No, they didn't. He never approved of her lifestyle and was vocal with his disapproval. And she didn't like how he treated me—that she only said to me. The truth is, I always felt she feared him. I can't imagine why. Even with all his power issues, he was a good guy—he really was."

Yeah, right. Sure he was.

Zen fidgeted and coughed.

I leaned forward. "Was your daughter surprised about the gift?"

"No, not really. In fact, she showed no interest at all. If I recall correctly she was in a hurry to collect her daughter from pre-school and left shortly after."

"Why in the world would Simon accept a gift of tea from a complete stranger and begin using it?" I asked. "Wouldn't he be suspicious of it?"

Bev showed her perfect teeth. "Oh, he was—at first. So he tried it out on my cat."

My eyebrows shot into the air. Zen frowned and pushed back her Stetson. "He was ready to sacrifice your cat?" she said, bug-eyed.

"Yeah, well. That was Simon."

"I take it the cat had no problem."

"None at all. I'll be bringing her down with me on my next trip. And when my cat, Dolly, was fine, Simon was overly thrilled that he had an anonymous friend who was so thoughtful as to send him the tea. Every time he made a cup he puffed up with importance. *I,* he said, never got gifts from secret admirers. It was weird how receiving the gift made him feel so special and drinking it even more so."

Wow! Talk about an egomaniac. Totally over the top!

I could see that Zen was working hard at keeping her mouth shut.

I cleared my throat. "So other than Simon's open disapproval with your daughter, they never had any other harsh words or disagreements?"

Bev smiled slightly. "Simon was not the type of person you chose to fight with. He had a way of belittling people. I learned that early in my marriage. That's why I let him walk all over me." She shot a look at Zen who seemed to be trying her hardest to not open her mouth. "Don't look so surprised, Missy. I knew what my hubby was doing. I just didn't and still don't wish to live in a state of constant upheaval and drama. Peace is much more my choice. Besides, it made the poor man happy to think he was the king of his roost."

Zen looked at me, started to open her mouth, but zipped it again. Thank goodness.

"I understand you filed for a divorce?"

"I did. Simon was none too happy about that. But when he realized his settlement would be more than generous, he signed the papers."

"But why did you travel down here sharing the same cabin when you knew you were getting a divorce?"

"I suppose many would think that odd behavior. Simon was all about appearances. He didn't want anyone to know we were getting a divorce until it was all over. We were making this trip to make decisions as to who got what from our Florida home. Something that needed to be done.

Besides, train cabins have twin beds. I could care less about playing out the game for a few more days. I was so relieved he wasn't contesting."

"We understand that Simon also had a falling out with his brother. Could you tell us what that was all about?"

"Oh that. Sure. Simon's brother always had his hand out. Money ran through his fingers like melting ice cream. When Simon finally refused to keep giving him money, John left in a huff and I don't believe Simon ever heard from him again. I know I didn't, until this of course."

"I see. Were you aware of Simon's stand on the annexation issue going on here?"

"Sure. Simon stood with those who were against it. He said, like them, he wanted things to remain as they were. I was proud of him for that stand."

"Did you know that Simon was CEO of a real estate company?"

"Simon? A CEO? No I didn't. He never mentioned that to me."

"You never heard him talking about building high rises or condos?"

"I certainly never did. But Simon did keep secrets. His home office door was always closed. He could have been doing anything in there and I wouldn't have known it."

"Did your first husband have any dealings with Simon?"

"Forest? Why no. I don't think they ever met. Why would they? I was divorced from him years before I met Simon. And Diane certainly would not introduce them. She despised Simon. She loved her dad. He's a golf pro and she knew that Simon didn't think much of that profession."

I knew that Zen wanted me to bring up the tryst subject, but I looked at her and shook my head. When the waitress stopped at the table with the check I gave Zen some bills and asked her to pay at the register. With arms on table I leaned toward Bev. "How well do you know Breece Devino?"

Bev blinked several times and licked her lips. "How did you find out about him?"

Just as I suspected—VERY well. I was more than glad I had sent Zen out of earshot. I didn't even want to think what she might say or do when she heard Bev's confession.

"That's not important. I assume you and he were having an affair?"

Bev took a sip of her juice then nodded.

"How long was it going on?"

"Is this really any of your business?"

"It is if Breece decided to get rid of his competition."

"Oh, he would never do that. He's a prince. Doesn't have a violent gene in him. Well, if you must know, we've been seeing each other for about eight months now."

"Did Simon know?"

"Simon and I had an open marriage, but I would never participate in a threesome—never. Moon must have been enjoying getting under Zen's skin."

I could see that—most definitely. "Any chance after you filed for a divorce that Simon thought it was because of Breece?"

149

Bev's eyes flicked around the room. "Yes, that might have occurred to him. Yes, it's possible."

"But neither mentioned they had had a confrontation about it?"

"No."

"You kept the relationship secret from others in Matlacha. Why?"

"People are not as open-minded as Simon and I. Besides, what has my sexual life have to do with others? It's my business, not theirs."

"Ever occur to you that Breece might have sent that package of tea? Him being a knowledgeable herb and plant geek and all."

"Breece would never have taken the chance that I might drink some of that tea. Breece and I are in love. After he gets his divorce, we plan to marry. Diane loves him."

Ah, poor naïve Zen.

"So your daughter knew of your affair?"

"Oh, yes, she met Breece several times. They hit it off from the first. In fact, she's encouraged the divorce and marriage. She knows I'm not a lone wolf. I'm much more comfortable with a companion living with me."

"Do you have any idea of who might have wanted your husband dead?"

"The police asked that. But no, I really don't."

I thanked Bev, gave her my phone number, asking her to call if there was anything she remembered that she thought would help our case. She agreed.

I stood and waved to Zen to follow.

As we walked out, Zen lowered her voice. "Did you ask about the try . . ."

I stopped her. "Yes, and she denied it—very convincingly I would say."

"So what else were you talkin` about? You both seemed to have lots to say."

"Nothing of importance to the case."

Zen put her hands on her hips and glared at me. "You're lyin`, girl. You talked to her about Breece, didn't you? You don't want me to know how she answered. You think I can't take it."

"You sure you want to know?"

Her face reddened. Turning, she stomped off toward May Street.

"Zen!"

Without looking at me, she gave me the finger. I thought about going after her, but instead, headed in the opposite direction for the inn. I planned to question Breece in two hours. Hopefully, by then, Zen's anger would be spent and she would meet me in my room where Breece said he wanted to meet. If not, I'd conduct the interview on my own.

I decided I would spend the next hour and a half in a kayak. Paddling out on my own was almost as relaxing and as good thinking time as walking or going to a beach. Mostly I would head for a not-too-distant mangrove island and find an inlet where I could rest my paddle, put my legs on the sides of the kayak and drift in peace.

After renting the kayak I slid it into the water and wading, hopped into it, making sure I didn't land off-balanced. Nothing more embarrassing than tipping into water hardly deeper than my ankle. I'd done that a couple times when I first learned. I didn't plan to repeat the experience.

Dipping the paddle in and out of the Pass, I swung to the left, moving within fifteen feet from the back of several colorful cottages, a small motel and the bait shop. The water was calm, the sky cloudless. I inhaled deeply through my nose, letting air out my mouth. Dipped in again. And again.

Shouts. Sounds of breaking wood. I sat up straight. Three people were scuffling on a dock—one man, two women. To my surprise, it was the Amish women and Breece. One woman held a bat-sized piece of wood over her head. Breece ducked, causing the woman to almost fall into the water. The other woman grabbed for her friend. I paddled fast. Banging into the dock, I grabbed hold of a metal cleat used for tying up a boat just as Breece and the woman hit the water. I pulled myself up. The first attacker was bent over the side offering her hand to the other woman who was pushing Breece's yellow hair under the water.

"Hey! Let him go! What are you doing?" I yelled.

The woman on the dock swirled and backhanded me in the face. I spun around and went down on one knee. In less than a second my hands went up Karate-style and the fight began. Her spins and kicks were vicious and meant to damage. Mine were meant only to down her. Wham! Foot to head. Backward flop into water. As I shook my head and grabbed for the dock, I heard running feet. A quick glance told me it was Gator. I hauled myself up and over the planking. The two women disappeared around the cottage before I had time to crawl across the planks. Gator and I pulled Yellow Hair out. He wasn't breathing. Laying him out flat, telling myself I wouldn't get lockjaw, I applied mouth-to-mouth resuscitation. After several seconds, his chest moved. He coughed. Water burst from his lips. I sat back to catch my breath. Rubbing blood from the side of my cheek, I looked at Breece. He didn't look so good but he was alive.

Gator stood, then came down on one knee again. "What happened here?"

"Call an ambulance," I hissed, holding my ribs. "I don't know how long he was out."

Breece groaned. Gator scratched his beard. "I don't have a . . ." Distant voices made him turn. He placed his hands on either side of his mouth and yelled, "Hey, call an ambulance. NOW!" A cormorant spread its wings and shot away.

I grimaced.

"You take one to the gut?" Gator asked.

I nodded and gritted my teeth. "Maybe cracked a rib." I struggled up from the dock.

"You should stay put. Who did this?"

As a wave of nausea passed over me, I sat again and half-smiled. "Two of the prettiest, sexiest, black belt Amish women I've ever met."

Of course the medics could do nothing for me. A cracked rib just takes time to mend, but Breece and I were both taken to the hospital to have x-rays to make sure we had no broken bones. We didn't. As we waited for Zen to bring my car to the entrance from the parking lot, ignoring the pain I felt every time I moved and swallowing a groan, I broached the subject of Bev. "I spoke to Bev Hill."

"Yeah? So?"

"You don't want to come clean?"

"So we're havin` an affair, so what?"

"And you didn't tell me because?"

"Duh! How soon after that would it take for you to put me on the top of your suspect list? Like, ten seconds?"

"Maybe five."

"Case closed."

"Not exactly closed. Let me hear you say one more time that you did not kill Simon Hill." I took in a deep breath and winced.

He didn't look at me. "I did not kill Simon Hill. Why should I? He was goin` to be out on his ass soon. She was divorcing him and marrying me."

"So she said."

"She did? She admitted it?" He smiled. "That's cool. Yeah, I like that." He ran his hand through his greasy hair.

I kept my groan to myself.

27

Zen pulled up in my car in front of me and Breece, jumped out and opened our doors.

"Hey, girl, I'm sure you know, this car isn't safe. The driver's seat rocks more than a toy horse," Zen said.

"Yeah, I know. I just want it to last the season then I'll junk it. Breece, you sit in the back with me."

"Good luck with that," Zen said under her breath. "Hey what am I, your chauffer?"

"I got questions for him."

Zen glared at me in the rearview mirror.

Before we were at the first stop light, I asked. "Who were those women?"

Breece put his hands on his head bandage.

"I assume," I continued, "they're not Amish."

"You got that right." He dropped his hands.

"Are they the two women who needed money?" Zen gave him a look through the rearview mirror that added "jerk."

Wondering what was going on between them, I frowned.

"Yeah," he said.

"What money?" I asked.

"I'll tell you about that later," Zen grunted. "Ain't real important."

The crease between my eyebrows deepened.

"Why were you fighting?"

He glanced at Zen, lowered his voice and said to me, "We had an argument over some money I borrowed from Zen. It has nothin` to do with Hill's death."

Hmm.

"They your sisters you talked about?" Zen spit out.

"Yeah," he said slowly. "They're my sisters." Then he added quickly, "But not by blood. They're my step-mom's kids. They have this thing about travelling around the country in disguise. It's like a joke to them, foolin` people."

Oh, sure, I believed that. Like NOT!

"And they came to Florida for a family visit?" I asked.

"Not exactly. They hunted me up `cause they needed cash."

"For what?" I asked.

"To pay off a loan shark."

Now, that I believe. "And you wouldn't give them money so they decided to kill you?" I added. "Nice family."

Breece looked at Zen. "I gave them all I had, but it wasn't enough. They exploded! Both of them. Well, I guess Jessie saw what they did. As I said, we're not related by blood. They were brought up on the low side of the social scale—real low. My step-mom was a heroin addict. My pop left her not long after they married."

"But you kept in touch?" I said.

"Only with the girls. I felt sorry for them."

I switched subjects. "What's your connection with Arcadia?"

His eyebrows shot up. "Arcadia? That's where my oleander buyer lives. Why?"

"Just wondered. The town keeps coming up in conversations about the case."

"You plan to press charges against them girls?" Zen asked.

"My sisters? Hell, no! Why would I do that? It was just a family squabble." He stomped on the floor, bent over and lifted the mat. "Wow! This car defines junker. That's daylight down there."

"Whatever." The car hit a bump. I touched my ribcage, controlled a groan, and readjusted my body. "And *my* part in this little family fight?" I asked.

He dropped the mat. "Too bad you saw us and interfered. They wouldn't have drowned me. They get mad fast, but they get over it fast too."

So much for expecting a thanks.

"Remind me," I grouched, "not to come to any more of your family reunions."

Zen gave Breece another angry look and spun the wheel, knocking me and him into the doors.

I caught my breath. "Hey, take it easy, Cowgirl. This car has two tires in the graveyard."

"More like three."

"And my ribs are screaming."

"Oh, sorry. Dang. I forgot." She turned and looked back at me. "You okay?"

"She meant to have my head hit the window," Breece said. "Women just don't have any sense of humor."

Knowing Zen well, I braced my feet against the back seat to keep myself steady.

The car swerved again. Breece's head cracked against the glass. "Damn, girl! Chill!"

I closed my eyes and put my head back. Just get me home, I was thinking. Just get me home.

As the miles passed, and I listened to Zen and Breece's hostile exchanges, I couldn't help notice that Zen seemed to be making a point not to bring up Bev Hill. I wondered if Breece felt guilty. Some people's guilt button was easy to push, others were rusty and sealed shut. My button was well-greased.

"Here we are," Zen said.

I pushed away my thoughts. Breece climbed out. I opened my door, almost swallowing my tongue. "Ohmigod!" A figure in a full black chador stood at the entrance to the inn with her back to us. "Bahar?"

After the bathroom horror, the next day Bahar and her mother had flown back to Iran without a word of farewell. I shook my head. Poor Bahar. Living the rest of her public life totally covered in black. The poor little girls who were killed in the auto accident later. If only . . .

The woman turned. Her penetrating green eyes held my gaze so long I felt hypnotized. But no, this was not Bahar. Of course not Bahar.

An olive-skinned man in a white shirt and khaki's came out of the office, smiled and nodded at us. He took the woman's elbow and they headed for the back of the inn.

I closed my eyes and stayed put for several seconds. One had to always be ready for surprises—emotional or otherwise, Grandma Murphy said . . . One never knew.

Zen asked if I was okay again. I said good, just a little shaky. She walked me to the door and I assured her I'd be fine.

After Zen and Breece took off, I went into my room and had a talk with Gar.

"Where do you think Bahar is? Married in Iran? Yeah, most likely."

I stood up and paced, focusing on the loose links in the case, then returned to consulting Gar.

"There's no way Shirin is going to tell us what was in the package, is there? Or if she does make up some story, how can we believe her? We can't, of course."

I patted Gar's head. "We've learned a bunch of stuff, but none of it proves anything. Everyone we interviewed had a motive for killing Hill. Several had opportunity. All had means. But we're no closer to knowing who the killer is, are we? Maybe this will be one of those unsolved cases? Hawk says there are a lot of them. Maybe it's because people like Hill spent most of their lives making enemies so there are too many potential killers smart enough to leave minimal clues?"

I sat on the edge of the bed and fought with my brain. Then, gazing steadily at him, I set my feet squarely onto the floor.

159

"Maybe, just maybe we've been going about this all wrong. Maybe the killer is not in Matlacha. Maybe Hill has other enemies evil enough to send him poison, not caring whether his wife or step-daughter or friends were killed if served. That would be a whole lot of evil and hate."

Arcadia—an hour away? Or Boston—a plane ride away?

I tapped the top of the nightstand, then took out my iPad and looked up Richard Rancine of Arcadia's number and made the call. His wife answered. He wasn't at home and wouldn't return for three days. Turned out he was a master gardener who specialized in oleander varieties. I set down the phone. The story Breece had given Zen checked out. Where could we glean the most information, obviously not Arcadia—not for three days anyway—not until Rancine returned.

"Boston it is," I told Gar.

28

Helen, Gator and I arrived at my trailer for our poker game at the same time. After everyone got their drinks, we took our seats. I didn't expect Breece to show up, but when he did, although I was tempted, I didn't throw him out. He didn't speak as he slid into the empty chair.

"Your deal," I said, shoving the deck across the table at him.

Not looking at me, he began to shuffle.

Helen and Gator glanced at each other. "Something wrong between you two?" Gator asked.

"Nah," Breece and I said.

"Good. Then deal."

Gator won the first pot. Me, the second. It was my deal.

"How's the investigation goin`?" Gator asked.

"It ain't," I said.

"Really? Seems like I'm hearin` you're askin` lots of questions. You must have learned something."

"Yeah. Mostly we're finding out that lots of people are sleepin` around and keepin` it a secret."

Helen slammed her cards on the table. "Zen!"

I began to deal. "Chill, girl. I wasn't talking about you and Hill."

Breece stood. "Anyone want another beer?"

Gator and Helen said sure. Breece headed for the fridge, but kept talking. "Zen was referring to me. In case you're wonderin`. Bev Hill and I plan to get hitched."

I closed my eyes. Didn't realize words could hurt so much.

"Well, that ain't right," Gator said.

"Just what ain't right about it?" Breece asked. "You think I'm not good enough for her?"

Gator spit a wad of tobacco in a Mason jar before answering. "Guess I thought you had feelings for another woman."

"Well, I don't. And if any woman thought I did, that's her problem. Bev and I've been seeing each other for months. She was planning to divorce him for me."

Helen began to laugh. I opened my eyes. Breece whirled on her. "What's so funny, girl?"

"Simon was planning to leave Bev for me." Helen shook her head. Tears of sadness ran down her face. "Isn't that rich? The wife is leaving him for you. And the husband for me?"

Breece opened a beer, tossed the cap into the wastebasket and took a long swig, then set it on the counter.

"No wonder you've been so frustrated at Hill all these months. Your anger. It had nothing to do with the annexation, did it?" Helen said.

Breece yanked open the fridge and pulled out three more beers.

"How come I never knew you was married and having a fling?"

Breece shrugged. For some reason I couldn't put my finger on, the stiffness of his spiked hair irritated me—made me want to grab it and give it a pull. Why was I attracted to such a lyin`, thievin` druggy? What the hell was the matter with me?

"Guess there's a lot about this guy the two of us never knew," Gator said, eyeing Breece.

"Make that three," Helen said.

I snatched a beer from Breece. "Are we goin` to play cards, or what?" I asked, trying not to show that I was fuming and really, really hurting.

After dealing, I asked, "So those sisters of yours wanted more money, did they?"

Breece didn't look up from his cards. "Yeah, but I'm sure they've left the area by now. They wouldn't like it that someone saw them on the dock and cops are involved. They're shy around the law."

"Yeah, I just bet they are," I said. "Must be a family trait."

I spent the night watching Breece's poker face with different eyes. No doubt about it, he was a damn good player.

29

The next day, Zen and I cozied up to the bar at Bert's. "You think we're beatin` up the wrong bush?" Zen repeated.

"Yeah, I'm thinking we focused all our efforts on people in Matlacha and got nowhere. It's time to broaden our scope."

Zen's eyes lit up. "Like go to Boston?" This was a trip she'd been hoping for ever since the case had begun.

"Yeah. Like go to Boston."

Zen tore her Stetson off and tossed it into the air. "Hot damn!" she yelled, causing wide-spread laughter in the room.

I waited for her to settle down before continuing. "Hill seems to have made enemies wherever he landed. I'd like to talk to his brother and visit that real estate company that Bev seems to have not known about. Maybe even talk to his step-daughter."

"And I get to go, right?"

"Of course."

Zen's grin could have lit up a darkened closet.

"Simon Hill angered one evil dude," I added.

"Why evil? Anyone could kill if provoked."

"Yeah, but this person didn't care how many were killed to accomplish the mission. Hill could have offered a cup of tea to his wife, step-daughter, or, ohmigod, even offered a sip to his grandchild. Good lord, this could have been a serial killing."

"Eww. I never thought of that."

We were silent as I let that sink in.

"You don't think that was the killer's purpose, do you?" Zen asked.

"I don't know, but we need to keep in mind that this killer is capable of anything. We need to stay on our toes."

"Yeah, the killer would be a damn good, evil poker player," Zen said.

"One thing that occurred to me last night."

"What's that?"

"If the tea didn't kill Bev's cat but it was confirmed it killed Hill, how did that happen?"

"Switched?"

"Maybe. But by who?" I sat at the table. "I'm thinking we need to fly to Boston soon. Can you get time off?"

"You bet I can. Just let me know when."

I spent the evening on my iPad researching Hill's company and getting air tix.

30

We left the following night. Tix were pricy, but not my problem. Shirin's cousin had said spare no expense when she hired me.

As a surprise to Zen, I booked our return trip two days later than I assumed we'd need for our investigation. After all, she had never seen Boston and although we were staying with an old friend of mine since my apartment in Cambridge had been rented for the winter, I hoped we would have time to visit my mom and grandma. It wouldn't do to be that close to them and not make the effort. If they found out, I would never hear the end of it. Both had expressed hopes that one day they would meet some of the people I talked about from Florida. I just hoped they would live through the experience of meeting my bling-studded, tattooed cowgirl southerner sidekick. I hadn't called them yet to warn them of our visit. It would have to be a last-minute deal. Who knew what would happen with the questioning and info gathering?

Taking Uber from Logan, we pulled up in front of the walk-up brownstone apartment building at 2 p.m. I'd never been at my friend Sam's new digs, so I was as surprised as Zen to see how charming the street was. Eight identical brick buildings circled the cul-de-sac. Geraniums were still in bloom. When I had last visited Sam she lived in a grungy apartment in Cambridge. This was definitely a step up. But then she was no longer a student. She now played Oboe for the Boston Opera. More than once she had told me that she had two extra bedrooms and I was welcome to use them any time. Both were rented, but neither was ever occupied as the Midwest tenants only rented the rooms so they'd have an address for their conservative, religious parents to send mail to. Neither wanted their folks to know they were living in sin with their boyfriends. When I conveyed this to Zen on the plane, she laughed until tears rolled out of her eyes, then ordered another beer.

Sam met us at the door to the building. We hugged. I introduced Zen. Sam welcomed her with warmth, then led us up to her second floor apartment all the while talking about her day and how great it was that we had come.

Sam and I had gone to college together. I'd lasted only one semester. I wouldn't have even made that if it weren't for my boyfriend, Will's insistence. Sam took being a student of music as her calling. Since she was three she'd played a musical instrument and achieving a degree in music had always been her dream. When I was nineteen I'd envied her drive, but trying to emulate her just hadn't taken. She'd stayed in college, getting her Master's degree while I played at drawing, then had let it slide until I had met Will Rolins. Just because college and studying art didn't take, didn't mean he didn't stop hounding me about taking my art seriously. He was a sweet guy, but it was hard for him to understand that work, real work, zapped your creative energy. He lived on a trust fund and enjoyed several adventure-packed hobbies, that is, until he was

167

murdered. But enough of such sad thoughts, here I was in Sam's home. So cool. Very cool!

Wood floors polished to perfection. A bay window wall. High ceilings. Dining room. Three bedrooms. Small fireplace. I was amazed. I stepped to the window and moving the curtain looked outside at a brilliant red-leafed tree. Stunning. Truly stunning. A husky man sat on a bench petting someone else's dog who was pulling on the leash to continue walking. I scratched an itch at the base of my neck and let the curtain fall.

"How can you possibly afford this?' I asked. "Even with two absentee roommates this has to cost a bundle. It's right off Mass. Ave. in the heart of Boston. Is the pay that good with the Opera?"

"Hah! Hardly. And you're right. I was lucky. When I put in my application, the owner needed someone to keep watch over the rooftop patio. He said if I would monitor its use, he'd cut my rent price. I jumped at the chance."

"Whoa! A rooftop patio?"

"Yeah. We'll have a drink up there later. It's a bit cool, but still doable. All that's expected for the reduced rent is make sure there's no conflicts over who's using it when. Only had one problem and managed to negotiate the two tenants into combining their parties. Turned out to be a blast, actually. Put your things in whichever extra bedroom you want. They're behind the kitchen there. Mine's at the other end of the apartment."

We got settled and met in the living room. Three wine glasses sat on a tray next to a bottle of Merlot. Zen asked for a beer. Sam smiled and

168

returned to the kitchen, soon bringing out an ale. Zen looked at the bottle in her hand and frowned. Sam poured her and me a generous portion of wine and we all clicked glasses to celebrate our reunion. After Zen took her first sip, her grimace was classic. "Don't got any Bud or Guinness, do ya?" she asked.

Sam laughed and nodding toward the kitchen, said, "Help yourself. Behind the milk on the top shelf."

Zen shot out of the room.

Sam raised her glass at me. "I like your friend. Very Florida."

"Yeah, Zen's a jewel. It was a lucky day when I met her. She's all excited to see some of Boston after we get our business done. I'm hoping we have time for that."

"When do you have to leave?"

It was Friday. We had until Wednesday.

"Wednesday morning."

"Well, if I have any free time I'd be happy to join you on any of your wanderings. But it's a busy weekend for me. We're getting ready for a concert."

"Hey, totally understand. We're playing the time by ear. We'll spend tomorrow trying to accomplish our business, but don't even know if that's possible."

"Well, feel free to stay here. I'll be rehearsing late. We should be able to catch each other for a nightcap each night, if nothing else."

"Perfect."

Zen re-entered.

Sam stood. "Let's take these to the roof. You'll love the view."

What was not to like about sitting on a rooftop that overlooked a park, a cobblestone corridor that Sam said went as far as Northeastern University and other historic buildings, surrounded by glorious late fall color? I mean, it didn't quite beat the water view I had in Florida. And it wasn't like it was warm enough for us to sit out, however it was spectacular nonetheless.

"So, I hear you're doing P.I. work as a side business to being a property manager and an artist?"

I set my glass on the ledge. "Yeah, I guess that sums it up."

"For someone who always hated snow, the cold, and the ice, you've done a fine job of creating a life to avoid such dreaded things."

I chuckled. "Yeah, I guess I have."

Zen raised her beer and asked if we needed more wine. We both agreed and without another word, she opened the door and headed down to the apartment.

"So, is P.I. work dangerous?"

I shrugged. "Can be." The face of the Amish women flashed in my mind.

"If you don't mind me asking, what's the case you're working on now all about?"

"Boston businessman poisoned with a perfect cup of oleander tea."

"Ah, come on. Don't pull my leg. Sounds like a B-rated TV mystery."

"If you think about it, most tellie murders are B-rated. It isn't the murder that adds the "don't turn the channel" thrill. It's the twists and turns that happen as the sleuth is solving the crime. And the characters of course. Viewers want to connect with the characters."

"Hmm, I suppose. Hey, something I've always wondered."

"Yeah?"

"Did you ever hear from that Iranian friend of yours who went back to Iran?"

"Nope. Never did. Why?"

"Oh, I always noticed that when she and those kids came up in a conversation, you ended up crying. Just wondered if you ever talked to anyone about your feelings."

"She came up in conversation?"

"Only when you had a couple more drinks then you should have."

I looked out at the lights of the city. "Oh! Right. No, I never got professional help or anything."

Sam was not the first person who had suggested this. Hawk, my grandma and my first boyfriend had all done the same. But I buried it. Who had time or money to see a shrink?

Zen's head popped through the door. She had put her Stetson back on and replaced her travel blouse with a bling low-cut sleeveless number. Her snake tat rippled. What would mom and grandma think of Zen? Hah! They'd love her.

"Look at this woman! What's not to love?" I said, purposefully changing the conversation.

Zen frowned. "You pokin` fun at me?"

I chuckled and shook my head. "No way, Cowgirl. I'm dead serious."

Zen came to my side in two long-booted strides and threw her arm around my shoulders. I worked real hard at protecting my ribs.

I glanced at Sam. Our eyes caught. She raised her glass before taking a drink.

"God, I can't believe we're in Boston," Zen cooed. "Here, let me pour you two another glass. Where we goin` to eat? I'm starved."

31

At breakfast the next day after Sam left for rehearsal, Zen asked me to fill her in on why we were visiting the real estate company—as in, what did we hope to get out of it?

"Simon Hill was its CEO. According to Breece, the company was interested in building a high-rise on that parcel the Cape purchased."

"Yeah, but how would that connect to his murder."

"That's exactly the point. We don't know. We have to be diligent about following the clues and see where they lead us."

"Like bloodhounds?"

"Yep. Just like that."

"Once we talk to people there, will we have time to see the Common? I've always wanted to see the Hatch Shell and duck pond."

"We'll see. Don't get your hopes up."

Pouting just a tad, Zen finished her bowl of cereal while I swept the crumbs from my toast into my hand and dumped them into the wastebasket.

"I like your friend."

"She likes you too."

"Has she always been so straight-laced?"

"She's twenty-eight and plays the Oboe like an angel. She flirts mercifully with older men she will never date. She wears black and white exclusively. On Thanksgiving and Christmas she works in the homeless soup kitchen. She's generous to a fault. And she was raised by a single crack mom in the inner city of Chicago where she missed by two heartbeats joining a gang." I put my cup under the faucet and turned on the water. "Has she always been so straight-laced?" I glanced over my shoulder at Zen. "I'll let you answer that."

We stepped out of the taxi looking up at the twenty story building. "This it?" Zen asked.

Another taxi pulled up a couple car lengths behind us and honked his horn at a jaywalker. I glanced that way. My eyelids lowered. Why did the guy who had just exited the cab look familiar? But when he turned and walked in the opposite direction, I assured myself I was being paranoid and put him out of my mind.

We went inside and took the elevator to the sixth floor of a building that had lots of sparkle. Lots of modern class. The room we entered was filled with half walls—each cubicle occupied by one person and a computer on a small desk. Very not-Matlacha.

I looked around and spotted a closed door with the word "Office" on it. "Follow me," I said to Zen.

The heels of her boots clicked so loud heads popped up like toast in a toaster from several cubicles. Each time one erupted, Zen called out "Howdy" and tipped her Stetson.

"Behave yourself," I whispered.

She grinned and retorted, "Hah, this is way too much fun. These poor people need some entertainment. Look at this place. Good god! Where are the windows?" She smiled and tipped her hat at a man with thinning hair and glasses so thick they distorted his eyes. When we neared the door, Zen waved her hat again. I'm not going to say what she did with her bum. I hurried forward.

"Zen," I hissed, "I'm going to knock. You ready?"

Tucking her smile away she straightened her shoulders. "Let's do this," she said.

I knocked and opened the door when a woman's voice said to come in. She sat behind a large desk. Long-sleeved white blouse buttoned close to throat. Back arrow-straight. Hair pulled into a bun at her neck. And although her eyes had trouble disconnecting from Zen's pink, glittering jeans and red boots, she simmered that Mr. Voss would be with us in a few minutes and instructed us to sit, never once taken her eyes off Zen.

George Voss, who appeared to be somewhere in his sixties, put down a phone as we entered. Pin-striped suit. Black shirt. Red tie. Black hair. Green intelligent but shifty eyes. Manicured fingernails. Gold band on left hand. When he smiled, his mouth rose higher on the right side than the left.

His calculating gaze took my number more than once, but after one quick, disdainful glance, ignored Zen. He obviously didn't like Zen's get-up. I controlled my irritation.

We settled in the chairs six feet from the desk facing him. I crossed my legs. Zen pushed her Stetson back.

I spoke first. "Thanks for seeing us on such short notice."

He pushed a stack of papers to the side of the desk and said, "My pleasure. After spending the morning talking to fools and dealing with idiots, I appreciate the diversion." His smile was wide, but was more false than Zen's LV fake designer handbag she had left at home. His eyes had trouble leaving my girls. These type of guys made me want to puke.

I smiled inwardly and for another test of his personality and values, I crossed my legs. He noticed. It was my turn to inwardly sneer.

Zen withdrew a nail file from her colorful clothe purse that featured gators, flamingoes and pelicans and started filing her thumbnail.

"We understand that Simon Hill was your CEO?" I said, noting his face had become flushed.

"Ah, yes, poor Simon. What a tragedy. Hopefully his killer will be found soon. The police, of course, were here within hours of his death." He looked into my eyes, then at my girls again. "Did you know him, ah, personally?"

"No, afraid not. I did meet him and his wife on the train, but that was it. Actually, we've been hired to help find his killer. And, by the way, my eyes are near my nose, not between my arms."

The words took him off guard. It was a moment or two and several sweeps over us (more me than Zen) before he could speak. "Well, well," he finally said, "isn't life full of surprises. I would never have guessed you two were feminists. How, ah, charming. I admire strong women. Do feel free to ask me anything."

Zen switched her file to her pointer finger.

His eyes slowly inspected her. He didn't hide his look of scorn. I felt like slapping him.

"What kind of CEO would you say Simon was?" I asked.

"Oh, he was all business. Didn't have time for foolishness. This company is only four years new, but we're already showing promise of being rated near the top for sales and development and I attribute that all to Simon and his ruthless diligence."

"So, you thought he was ruthless?"

"When it came to getting this company where he wanted it to be, he was."

"Did he have enemies?"

"Plenty. You can't be competitive in the real estate business without making a lot of enemies."

"Any that would want him dead?" Zen asked.

He cut her a sneer. "Obviously."

Zen's eyes narrowed and she slid the file into her purse. I was more than glad to see that because I had a brief, sickening image of her sticking it into his hand.

Voss returned his attention to me.

"I assume you wouldn't mind giving us a list of those enemies?"

"I'll have my assistant draw one up and email it to you. That is, if you have email in Florida?"

I ignored his dig. Hoped Zen did as well. "I'll leave my address with her. Did you know his wife?"

"We met several times. She's a lovely woman, an excellent wife, and I understand, a loving mother and grandmother. I must admit I was a bit surprised to see that Simon had married such a woman. He so loved . . . but as I said, life is a surprise a minute."

"Loved what?" I asked.

"Younger, sexier, edgier women."

I thought of Moon McCain and Helen Lewis. Both fit that description.

"We understood Hill's wife didn't know about his being CEO of this company—or were we misinformed?"

"Not at all. Simon was adamant about not telling her, but that didn't mean we didn't socialize."

"I see. We understand there were plans to build a high rise in Matlacha, Florida," I said.

His eyebrows furrowed. He made a tower with his fingers. "I'm not sure what you are talking about?"

"Are you telling us your company had no plans to build a high-rise in Matlacha?" Zen's voice was gruff.

He refused to look at her. "Hmm, Matlacha, Florida, you say." His lips worked. "Mat . . . Oh, is that how you pronounce it. I always pronounced it differently. Oh, sure, if that's where you mean, yes, there was talk of such a project."

I leaned forward. "And?"

"There was a delay. Something about a problem with annexation, I believe. Yes, that's right. The project was put on hold." He looked thoughtful.

"Yes?" I asked.

"I just remembered what Simon said about the delay—something like—we'll just wait until a hurricane flattens those cracker's homes and wipes them out—they'll come begging for our help to get the tourists to come back."

"Obviously, Simon Hill was a very empathetic guy."

He looked toward the window. "Obviously. I suppose I didn't have to tell you that, but it does help you get a look at his personality."

I nodded agreement. "So Hill was upset the project was on hold?"

"He was quite upset about it. That high-rise would have made us a lot of money."

"I see." I looked at the plaque on his desk, then at him. "I take it you're the new CEO?"

"Temporarily, yes. The board needs to vote on the final decision, but I've been assured I'll keep the position."

Zen tapped her boot on the floor. "So Hill's death was real good for you," she said.

Voss did not acknowledge her words. He blinked once and focused on me, this time on my legs.

I swung my foot ever so slightly. "Were you and he friends?"

"Not really friends, as I said, but we did socialize on occasion."

"He was your boss?"

"Yes. Although I never thought of him like that. I've always owned a small share of the company. We were more like partners, with him owning the majority of the company shares, of course."

I slid back in my chair and nodded to Zen, giving her permission to do the Zen-thing she so loved doing. Her eyes sparkled. "We've been told Simon Hill had quite the unique way with some of those younger, sexy, edgier women."

Refusing to look at Zen, Voss almost suppressed a smirk.

She continued. "You ever join him in any of his sexual escapades?"

Voss shoved his chair back and jettisoned to a standing position. I was surprised to see he was no taller than five six. I was not surprised he didn't like the question.

"I take that as a yes," Zen said, joining me as I stood.

Lowering his head like a Spanish bull, Voss marched to the door and yanked it open. He didn't even bother to step back as we walked through.

"Guess he don't like me," Zen said with a grin.

"Nor the question," I added.

Zen stopped by the cubicle where the man with thick glasses worked, spoke to him, then joined me (after I left my email address and phone number with the assistant) at the elevator where she waved goodbye with her Stetson to all the other employees. When I looked back, the assistant was busy closing all the blinds on the windows of the office. I guess Voss was desperate for some consoling.

We stepped into the elevator.

"You think we'll get that list?" Zen asked.

"Not a chance."

"That's what I was thinkin`." Zen put her palms together and raised them prayer-fashion in front of her face. "Got time for the Common?"

I checked the time on my phone. "Just!"

Zen began clapping her hands and hopping up and down like a kid.

32

Ever since I was a toddler, one of my favorite Sunday afternoon treats was to go with Mom and Grandma Murphy to the Charles River where we would listen to a free concert in the Hatch Shell, walk the flowered paths, and if I was lucky, get to ride a Swan Boat. Not once did we leave without feeding the mallards. One of my most loved bedtime stories became *Make Way for Ducklings*. I was probably as excited as Zen to be going there. I just didn't show it.

"Come on," I said. "It's this way. The Swan boats won't be in operation this time of year, but the ducks will be there."

Zen, maneuvering around people, skipped and whirled along the sidewalk as I made a phone call to Hawk. "You have time to meet Zen and me at the Commons near the Swan boat dock?" I asked. He said he would be there in twenty minutes.

I pocketed my phone. "My ex-boss is going to meet us there."

"Yee haw! Hawk! Holy crap! I can't believe this! The Commons *and* the phantom Hawk!"

I was sure if Zen hadn't had on her cowgirl boots and a quilted coat she would have done a cartwheel. I shook my head and quickened my pace, hoping the increase of stride would help settle her emotions.

"I can't wait to tell Gator. He's goin` to be so-o-o jealous! Hey, hurry up, will ya?"

The Common was alive with crimson, gold, orange, yellow and green foliage. People in jackets and gloves strolled by, almost everyone with a look of pleasure on their face as they took in the late autumn leaves. I almost felt like we were walking through an oil painting. November could be a tricky month weather-wise in Boston, but the weather now was crisp with blue skies and only a slight breeze.

I sidled up to a cart and bought two bags of duck food from a tall, broad shouldered vendor wearing a knit cap and half-gloves who kept his head down. The hairs on the nape of my neck began doing their itch thing again. I eyed the vendor, but another customer crowded in and Zen was ruthless with her joy. I gave a bag to her and she dashed toward the pond. When I turned around, the vendor and his cart were gone.

"Hey, girl!"

Hawk! All six-foot-four, blue-eyed, blonde-haired Hawk. Even as tall as I was, he had to bend over to give me a proper hug (that didn't hurt enough to groan) and kiss on the cheek. How was it that he always smelled so good? I smelled like yesterday's laundry by midday. He held me at arm's length. "Too soon for the Florida sun freckle explosion?"

I raised and lowered my eyebrows at him. He laughed. "How's the neck?"

"All better." I kept my rib injury to myself.

He stepped back. "Good. Now, where is she? Hunting for a fishing rod?"

I nodded toward the pond. Zen was tossing food amidst a gaggle of mallards. Two other women dressed in parkas and fashionable knee-length boots were doing the same.

Hawk's eyes lit up like a bathroom scented candle. "The one with the Stetson?"

"You got it!"

"Hah!" In long strides he headed her way.

Stopping at another vendor's cart, I bought two more bags of feed then started toward my friends. They were laughing at the ducks vying for food.

"Oh, look at her. That momma took that right out of the duckling's beak!" Zen said as she spied me coming their way. "Oh, Jessie, I just love this place—all the statues, the history—so damn cool. Except for the cold weather, how in the world do you leave it?"

"Same question I ask her every year," Hawk said.

I handed Zen another bag of treats. "I'm a lucky woman. I have two places I love—each very different, both filled with topnotch friends," I said.

Zen and Hawk smiled at each other. Oddly enough, Zen wasn't flirting with him. Instead, she seemed in awe of his presence.

I wanted Zen and I to hear what Hawk had to say about the suspect list I'd given him, so I suggested we walk to a nearby coffee shop.

"But I want to go ice skating over at the Frog Pond," Zen whined. "I can see they rent skates."

I laughed. "If we have time, but first—business."

Zen walked backwards as we led her to the shop. Like, was she afraid the Frog Pond might disappear or something?

Hawk and I ordered an Espresso. Zen—hot chocolate with extra whipped cream. We chatted for a few minutes before I said, "Okay, give us the dirt."

He eyed me, then pulled out his iPhone, "You do remember I insisted that I was done being your information gatherer, right?

My face reddened. I nodded.

Looking irritated, he punched in his security code, scrolled then began to read:

"No. 1. Shirin Raab is a convicted murderer. Husband was murdered in a burglary. She was convicted of killing the shooter years later."

"Check," Zen said.

Hawk raised one eyebrow, pressed his lips together then looked at his phone again.

"No. 2. The victim, Simon Hill was a big time shyster who screwed anyone he met, both financially and sexually. Married only once. He started a real estate company four years ago and was being investigated by the feds for embezzling money from the company."

"That last part we didn't know," I said.

No. 3. Breece Devino has no record, used to work for an herb company, performs music around Matlacha and other places in Southwest Florida. Has no debt. No mortgage."

Zen interrupted. "Siblings?"

"None. He does have a wife and two kids who live in Georgia. Lists himself as self-employed."

Zen and I looked at each other. I assumed transmitting the same thought: So Breece lied to us about those women. Then, who were they?

Hawk continued. "No. 4. Helen Lewis has two DUIs and four maxed-out credit cards. Never married. Worked as a house cleaner her entire adult life."

He looked up. We said nothing. He went back to his phone.

"No. 5. Moon McCain is a former basketball player who now works as a plumber. Pays off her credit cards at the end of each month. Never married. No record.

"No. 6. Paul Lowinsky is a retired Bible salesman. Minor drug abuse as a teen. Married four times. Divorced by all. Listed as a sexual predator."

"Damn," Zen said.

Hawk continued. "Got caught with sixteen-year-old daughter of last wife. Served his time and became "born again" in prison."

"Oh, he's born again, all right," I said, not bothering to erase the sarcasm from my reply.

"And last but not least, Beverly Hill. You already know most of this. Heiress to a real estate fortune. Married twice. First husband was golf pro, Forest Johnson, and the father of her only child, Diane. Nasty divorce after three years where the pro took Bev for all he could get."

Odd. Bev said her daughter was close to her dad. What daughter would be close to such a guy?

Hawk continued. "Hill was her second husband. She filed for a divorce from him a month ago. Been married to him for ten years. The lesbian daughter Diane has an adopted kid. Oh, but nada on the two nameless Amish women." He set down his phone. "That's all I got, ladies."

"Thanks," I said. "Any chance you know anything about the current Hill and Hill Properties, LLC's CEO, George Voss?"

"Nah, but it won't be hard for you to get his info." His expression went serious, stern, father-like. "As you know, all the information I gathered could have been collected by you."

I looked down at the table. How many times had he said this to me?

"It's more than time for you to end your dependence on my skills. You are more than capable of gathering information."

Dang. Here we go again.

He looked at Zen. "I've been at her for the past six months to do her own work. She doesn't need me anymore, but she won't listen."

Zen pushed back her Stetson. Her eyes barreled into me. So did Hawk's.

Double dang.

"Hey, I'd miss you," I said, trying to make light of his comment.

His expression hardened. "So, miss me." He stood.

I blushed.

He pointed in the direction of the pond. "Those ducklings back there? They got to learn to swim on their own. Dependence isn't the ticket to success and I'm more than overworked." He reached out his hand to Zen.

"Real nice to meet you, Zen. Hope to see you again." He glanced at me. "Next time you contact me, make it a pleasure call." And he walked away.

I could have cut the silence at the table in two with one string of a cobweb.

Minutes later, with me still in shock, Zen stood and I followed her on a path.

"Any chance Hawk's push for your independence has anything to do with you doing all the self-reflecting, P.I. improvement thing?" Zen asked.

I looked away.

Zen continued. "He's right, you know. How many times do you have to be told you're a damn good P.I.? Where's your self-confidence, girl?"

My shoulders hunched forward. I felt like that bird shit under the tree. "Whatever."

The path took a turn.

I raised my chin in defiance and didn't answer. Hawk's sudden rejection was hard to take and even more irritating because he had done it in front of Zen. Of course I could have done the research on my own. But . . . still . . . My chin lowered. I was still worried about making mistakes, mistakes that could cause . . . I kicked a stone out of my way.

We passed the Visitors Information Center. "Hey, what's that red stripe all about?" Zen asked, pointing at the sidewalk.

"It's the beginning of the Freedom Trail," I said in a distant voice.

Zen was right. I'm a human who can't escape her past. The best I could do was to try to rise above.

A nearby tree shimmered in autumn hues of red. Sunbeams split the leaves in two. The image was breathtaking. I looked into the azure sky. A cloud drifted toward the east. An eagle soared into the tree. "Okay, okay, I get it," I whispered.

Although I wasn't a practicing Catholic, that didn't mean I didn't believe in God and his (or her) mysteries. Sometimes it was like God was everywhere sending out messages for me to get or not get. I felt all this sparkling beauty was a cosmic snap of the fingers—a reminder to think positive and to accept my need to change.

With effort, I straightened my shoulders and pulled the door shut to the hurt of Hawk's rejection. I vowed not to let feelings of low self-esteem control me if I could help it. Easier said than done.

Finally, I said, "You're right, Zen. So is Hawk."

"Boy, you hit that nail on the head!'"

"Hey!"

Zen laughed and skipped ahead.

I caught up to her. "Hey, the Freedom Trail is only two and a half miles and goes by all the historic sites you're so excited about. You'll love it. We could have a beer at a pub near Faneuil Hall and eat anywhere along the way you wish. Want to walk it?"

Zen wiggled her shoulders. "Super cool! But after we ice skate right?"

We stepped out of the park.

Bam!

"Jesus, what was that?" Zen yelled.

Grabbing her arm, taking Zen with me, we hit the ground.

Bam!

Sirens sounded. People ran toward us. I raised my chin from the cold cement to see if we should be hightailing it. Cops, guns drawn.

"You hit?" one asked.

I looked at Zen. She looked at me. We shook our heads.

"Stay put," a cop yelled as she continued on.

A bird landed beside us.

"I'm gittin' up. It's cold down here," Zen said.

"No way, girl. Not 'til they tell us to."

My cheek chilled as we waited.

"Hey, it's way too, way, cold down here," Zen whined.

"I know. Just wait."

Crunch. Crunch.

"Okay, you two. You can get up now. Are you sure you're okay?"

"Did you get anyone?" I asked standing.

"Nah."

Two bullets were recovered from two tree trunks. One that I was standing in front of and one that Zen was. The shooter wasn't found. No one knew who was being shot at. So, after confessing to the cops that we were Florida P.I.s investigating a murder, they warned us to watch our backs and to call them if anything "funny" happened. Of course I didn't say that travelling with Zen, meant that something "funny" happened more often than not, but I was tempted to. Feeling a tad shaken, Zen and I headed back to Sam's brownstone apartment. After we shared our story with her, we agreed to order pizza in. Not that the incident made us nervous or anything. No way had we been the targets. Anyway, that's what we tried to convince Sam—and ourselves.

"So no Freedom Trail? No ice skating?" Zen asked.

"Let's give our sightseeing plans a rest for now, okay?"

Instead, I watched a bad movie on TV with my old college friend, Sam, then called it a night, deciding to make a list of chain of events. I don't know what Zen was doing in her room.

My list:

Met Bev and Simon on train near end of trip. Simon had gut ache.

Talked to Amish girls, saw Breece and talked to Shirin who said she was asked to leave dining car.

Felt tension in train when porter came into car.

Decided to go back to dining car to find out why Shirin would be excluded.

Porter barred my way.

Heard scream.

Amish girls used cell phone.

Saw Simon being taken away on stretcher.

As left train, the porter gave me a note from Hill asking to see me.

Decided to stop into hospital to see how Bev and Simon were doing and find out what he wanted.

Found out Hill was dead.

I stopped writing and read over my chain of events. One word stood out, "Porter". Hmm. I set down my pen and picked up my sketchpad and drawing pencil, closed my eyes, then opened them and began to draw.

Slowly, ever so slowly the face and upper body of the garage door-sized porter filled the page. Broad shoulders, beefy arms, square face, wide nose, bushy eyebrows—one higher than the other—scar over right eyebrow running into hairline. Neck same width as his head. With a few strokes I added his hair—longish in front swept to the right. Shaved on both sides.

Holding out my drawing pad, I inspected my work. I bit my lip, flipped the page and began to draw him in profile. When I was finished, once again I held out the pad at arm's length. I'll be damned. I'd seen this guy more than just the time at the train. He might have been the guy on the bridge in Matlacha who had pointed out the dolphin. He could have been the guy who had left the taxi in Boston when we arrived at the real estate office. Maybe even the vendor in the Common. He was most likely the guy who'd been following us so close that my neck hairs kept itching. But was he the person who shot at us? And how did he fit into this case?

33

I scratched my snake tat. I knew I shouldn't call him. Breece was spoken for. I knew that. But who cared? He was a friend and friends are allowed to call their friends when they're feeling upset. Just because he needed to steal some money wasn't really no skin off my nose and didn't make him no enemy. Just because he took drugs (and they were obviously not pot *and* not for his health) didn't make him all bad. Besides, once he's married, he'll change. Getting shot at today made me want to hear his voice.

He answered on the first ring, real friendly. I hugged my beer and nestled against my pillow.

"Yeah, man," I said, "this place is super cool. Tomorrow we're walking the Freedom Trail. Can you believe it? We're staying with Jessie's friend in Back Bay. Talk about a woman. You'd love this gal. Musical and talented Jessie says. Just like you."

"Good for you, girl. Where in Back Bay you stayin`?"

"Oh, the place is called Durham Street or Road or something. It's the perfect location, right off Mass. Ave. and it's a genuine, real deal brownstone. The apartment is on the second floor and Sam—her real name's Samantha of course—gets a break in rent `cause she helps take care of the rooftop patio. I really like her, but can't imagine her on our island."

Breece chuckled. "So I won't have musical competition, huh? What are your other siteseeing plans?" he asked.

"Oh, Jessie's playing that by ear. She says after we talk to Hill's bro and step-daughter we'll have time for some fun. I sure hope so. I want to try my luck ice skating in the Common."

"So nothing much else exciting happened today?" Breece asked.

I set the beer on the table. Should I tell him we'd been shot at? Is that something he should know? Nah! He'd just worry. I snatched up the bottle again. "Nah, nothing. Just a boring day talking to some old stuck up CEO. Just like you thought, Hill was a real a-hole."

After gab-boxing a bit more, I said goodbye and clicked the button.

34

It was after midnight when Zen tapped on my bedroom door and opened it a crack. "Can't sleep."

"Me neither. Come on in."

She settled on the foot of the bed. "So, do you think like me, that the killer's in Boston and knows we're here?"

I set down my sketchpad. "Could be," I admitted. "Who did you tell that we were coming to Boston?"

Zen sighed. "Only everyone I ran into in Matlacha."

"Oh course," I said, sighing.

"Sorry. I was just so excited."

"It's okay. I get it. I told Bev and after making that call, Shirin's cousin knew."

"Well, that's pretty much everyone involved in the case," Zen said. "We both know how news travels fast on the island."

"Yep."

"Did you call Hawk and tell him what happened?"

"Nah. What would be the point?"

Zen looked quickly at the floor. "What're we goin` to do about it?"

"First thing in the morning, we'll leave here. I don't want Sam in danger."

"And go where? Back to Matlacha?"

"No. We'll go to my mom's place. We'll be safe there. She lives in a fortress." I handed her my sketchpad. "Take a look at that guy and tell me if he looks familiar."

Zen stared at the page but said nothing.

"No? Turn the page."

After giving the profile a good look, she shook her head. "Nope. So who is he?"

"The porter on the train. I'm sure he was in Matlacha shortly after I arrived and I'm positive I saw him getting out of a taxi in front of the real estate office."

"So he's been followin' us?"

"Seems so."

"Think he shot at us?"

"Possibly."

"So how do we find out who he is?"

"First thing is to get this to the cops. He might have a record. Even if he doesn't, the cops need to know that this guy is following us, may have been our shooter, and may have something to do with Hill's death."

"What about talkin' to Hill's bro and step-daughter, weren't we suppose to meet them earlier this evening?"

"I called them and changed our meetings to tomorrow morning. We'll go to the cops after talking to them."

"So, we'll go walking the streets like nothin' happened?"

I flexed my shoulders. "I haven't figured that out yet. Got any ideas?"

She swung her leg up onto the bed. "Disguises."

I pulled my knees to my chest. "Go on."

Zen stood. "I'm havin` another beer to help me think." She hesitated. "You?"

I shook my head. Disguises were a stellar idea. But how would we accomplish that? If we left here to buy wigs or different clothes, we could be seen. Of course we could ask Sam to do that for us. As long as we didn't go with her, she should be safe. Still . . .

Sam rapped on the door. "Hey, listen, I can't sleep."

I motioned her in. Zen followed her. Sam's concerns were the same as ours. I showed her the drawings. She said she had never seen the guy but that he looked like a real Rambo. I enlightened her about Zen's idea and my decision to move. For some reason I couldn't put my finger on, I didn't tell her where we planned to stay. She assured us the move wasn't necessary, but not far under her words was relief. In the next second, her face brightened.

"I have just what you need. I helped with costuming for an amateur theatrical production last spring. I still have a box of clothes and wigs. They're in the storage room." She swiveled toward the door. "Come on!"

35

The next morning, Zen confiscated the bathroom first. As I waited for her to gussie herself up, I took out my drawing pencils and sketchpad and after looking at the porter's mug again, I finished the likeness of George Voss. Then I phoned Mom and (with misgivings) spilled the beans about our plans to stay with her, warning her to keep it a secret. She swore she would. I prayed that was true. Mom had a tendency to blurt out things she regretted in the next instant. You'd think Zen was her kid, not me.

The bathroom door opened and Zen walked out. Her hair was sectioned off with each part rolled in aluminum foil. A towel covered her shoulders. "I found this temporary dye in the box. This only takes half an hour and when you're tired of the color, it rinses out. This has got to be better than a wig. Besides, I've always wanted rainbow hair. Next!"

"But I heard you have to bleach your hair first!"

"You do, silly. That's what took me so long. I took a bath while I was waiting for the bleach to work."

I stepped around her, hoping the wigs I'd seen in the bottom of the box didn't look too fake. I really had no desire to bleach my red hair.

An hour and a half later when we existed the brownstone, Zen's frizzled purple, pink, blue and green hair made the newly fallen snow look dull in

198

comparison. We both wore spandex exercise leggings and skin-tight, low-cut shirts with orange and yellow running shoes. My wig was platinum blonde and styled in a severe tough rock star cut. Zen's vest was panther black, my fitted jacket was bright pink with white stripes. We looked like we belonged to a circus troop. But as long as we didn't look like ourselves, that was fine by me.

I had called Uber instead of a taxi. Maybe harder to follow? Not quite as conspicuous anyway. All I could think about was Mom and Grandma Murphy's faces when we arrived. Neither of them had anything good to say about women who dyed their hair. Mom's hair had turned grey when she was eighteen and Grandma Murphy said she was born with grey hair. "Why fiddle with what God gave us?" she often said in a threatening tone.

Zen, on the other hand, was too busy flirting with the driver to be thinking of anything else. I noticed (as did the driver) that her girls were kept in constant motion by her well-practiced yoga breaths.

I let Zen pay for the ride. It seemed only fair. She had the most fun. While she paid, I gave the street a once-over. Seeing no large Rambo-type character lurking anywhere, pulling Zen along, I headed for the steps.

As we traipsed up the stairs to the front door, I could hear the steel rods of four deadbolts slide back before the door flew open. In the next instant, Mom screeched and fainted at Grandma Murphy's feet as Grandma slammed her hands on her hips and gave me the evil stare.

Great. Just great.

Mom's house was narrow with three tiny bedrooms and a bath upstairs. Living room. Dining room, kitchen and mudroom downstairs. The living room was filled with overstuffed furniture, lamps with plastic covered shades, fake flower arrangements and bins filled with old magazines and newspapers yet to be read. All furniture faced the forty-two inch flat screen. The rectangular oak dining table was set with four plastic placemats and a dusty tulip bouquet in the center. The kitchen centerpiece was a chrome table with four chairs with red Naugahyde cushions. Every window was covered with maroon velvet drapes. Ever since I could remember, the back and front doors had so many locks I could take a nap while they were all unbolted. Mom was frail when it was convenient, on the paranoid side, and worried about everything from what the new volatile president would do next to whether her favorite TV show would go off the air before she'd had enough of it. Grandma Murphy had moved in after my dad had died. Grandpa had died several years before.

Grandma managed to bring Mom around and we helped her to the sofa. Grandma began fanning her face with a Good Housekeeping magazine while continuing to give me the evil eye. "Jesus, Mary, Joseph! Look what you've done to your mother. Shame on you. Whatever were you thinking? Coming here looking like a . . . well I won't even use the word in this house!"

"We're keepin' from being killed. That's what we're doin`," Zen blurted out, causing Mom to groan and bury her face in her hands.

"These here are disguises to keep us from being shot at. It already happened once!" Zen added.

I knew Zen thought she was helping, but if she kept at it, Mom was bound to faint again. When Grandma looked away, I mouthed to Zen to keep quiet. She rolled her eyes.

"Disguises?" Grandma said, looking more than relieved. "Great job, right Edy? Especially the fake snake tattoo."

Zen's face reddened.

Oh! Oh! I stepped in front of her.

"Want a beer?" Grandma asked.

Zen beamed. My shoulders relaxed. Mom's eyes seemed glued shut.

Later, after filling Grandma and Mom in on our investigation and what had happened in the park I pulled out the drawings and laid them on a table. No, they had never seen that face before. But, oh my, what a gangster's face. Should they call Cousin Tony to bodyguard us? No, no, I assured them. We would be fine.

Soon after, I slipped (I thought unseen) into Grandma's room and opened my grandpa's dresser—the item treated like an untouched shrine. I knew everything was kept as it had been when Grandpa was alive. Reaching in, I pulled out a pair of handcuffs, a small canister of pepper spray and an illegal stun gun and added them to my old high school backpack. Grandpa had always been ready for a break-in. I looked at the pistol. Yes, I had a carrying permit. But I hated packing a gun. But you are more than likely targets of a maniac, I told myself. I let out a big puff of air and grabbed the gun, made sure it was loaded and stuck it into the bottom of my bag.

Grandma stood in the doorway. "Where you think you're going with that stuff?"

"Got appointments we can't miss," I said, looking directly into her eyes.

Grandma began to speak, but Mom appeared behind her. "There is no way I'm letting you leave this house looking like that! What will people think?"

"But, Mom . . ."

Grandma interrupted. "We've been talking and we've got a better idea. Hang on!" And they hurried down the hall.

When they returned, they held up two of Great Grandma's flowered dresses, two of her wigs and two pairs of heavy-soled shoes. Grandma Murphy, of course, only wore black stretch pants and tight-fitting yoga shirts.

Great. Just great! We'll leave here looking like Great Grandma's card pals.

36

Neither Zen nor I were excited about conducting an interview decked out as elderly women, so we put the dresses over leggings and shirts and tucked extra shoes into our large multi-colored shopping bags provided by Mom. I, of course, was not allowed to take my backpack—far too youthful, Grandma assured me. So I tucked my goodies into the bag provided.

After arriving at the Back Bay address and ducking into an alley to change, we climbed several steps to double black doors. When we knocked, a woman appeared and we said who we were. She led us to the first room on the left of the narrow hallway.

Lester Hill, like his brother, had snow white hair, a clear complexion and a pleasant smile. His arms rested on the arms of the wheelchair he sat in. "Please take a seat. Ms. Murphy and Ms., ah, Zin, was it?"

We didn't corrected him.

The room was lined in filled bookshelves. The floors and expansive desk were dark oak. Oriental rugs had been placed in front of wing chairs facing the desk. Hill wheeled himself to the backside of the desk while Zen and I settled in the straight-back chairs.

"We are very sorry for your loss," I began.

He thanked me, folded his hands on the desk and waited.

"As I said on the phone, we've been hired to investigate your brother's death."

"Yes, and may I say that surprises me. Both Bev and I have absolute faith that the police will solve this dreadful business. Was it the insurance company who hired you?"

"No, and I'm afraid we cannot divulge that information. Client privilege."

Lester shrugged. "I assume Simon had a sizable life insurance policy. Perhaps his had a suicide clause that would negate the payment?"

I frowned. "You think your brother committed suicide?"

"My brother was a complicated man. Yes, I do think that was possible."

"Why?"

He ran his hand through his hair. "This was not well known. In fact, except for his doctor, I may have been the only one Simon confided in. He had pancreatic cancer. Was given one month to live and that was a month ago. Shortly after, he received divorce papers. I doubt he bothered to tell Bev."

I took some time to absorb that surprise before continuing, "Sounds like you and your brother had a good relationship."

"As good as could be expected under the circumstances."

"Circumstances?" I said.

"Simon put me in this wheelchair. Oh, it was an accident, of course. One of those teenage mistakes that happen when boys play around with a rifle. Although, shame on me, I always reminded him of his grin at the moment of impact." He managed a smile. "Brothers, you know? The bullet is lodged in my back. Too risky to take it out."

Zen and I gave each other a look. Then I leaned forward, "From our understanding, Simon was poisoned over several months. Do you really think it's possible he'd put himself through that much pain?"

"I assume he was on pain killers much of that time. I understand pancreatic cancer is quite painful. I wouldn't put it past Simon to try to frame someone for his death although he knew it was eminent. In his perverted mind it would be a way to maintain control of his demise from the afterlife—although I doubted he believed in one. Weird, but so very Simon."

"Was he really that evil?" Zen asked, leaning forward and fingering a frame. "Hey! I know this nursery rhyme! Simple Simon. Always loved it." She looked at Lester quizzically as if to say: What an odd thing for a grown man to have.

"Simon had this framed for me when I was about four. One of his bizarre, not-so-funny jokes. Go ahead and read it out loud. He was ten when he wrote it."

Zen started with a smile on her face, but that soon faded as she read:

Simple Simon met a DIE!! Man!!
Going to the fair.
Says Simple Simon to the DIE! Man,
Let me learn your ware.
Says the Die Man to Simple Simon,
Show me first your penny;

Says Simple Simon to the DIE! Man,
Indeed I have not any.
Simple Simon went a-fishing
For to slaughter and impale.
All the catch he had got,
were blood and guts gone pale.
Simple Simon took a hard look
at his brother's jawbone and gristle.
Eyeing his weaker skeleton very much,
caused clever Simon to smile, plot and whistle.

Zen's voice was barely a whisper by the end. My eyes were wide with disbelief. How disgusting.

"You asked if Simon was evil. My older brother who drowned my puppy when I was five? Who broke my arm when I was eight? Who shot me at point blank range when I was thirteen—accidently of course? You decide that for yourself. My brother liked pain, he liked lots of women, he liked to live on the edge—he had a bizarre sense of humor and loved his childhood nickname–Simple Simon. Although no one who knew Simon would think him simple in the least."

Zen, whose face was pale now, set the frame back on the desk.

"I keep that on my desk to remind me of who he always was. Perhaps getting cancer was poetic justice."

"Do you think he inflicted pain on his wife?"

George pressed his lips together before speaking. "I doubt if he did physically, but mentally and emotionally? Most definitely."

37

Zen and I left shortly after, leaving Lester Hill with my phone number. Looking first right then left, we ducked into the alley to change back into our Great Grandma clothes.

"I don't know about you, girl, but I'm not too keen on finding this guy's killer. Some people just deserve to die," Zen said as I zipped up her dress.

"I know what you mean, but we have to keep reminding ourselves we're doing this for Shirin's sake, not for his."

"Seems the autopsy should have listed his cancer," Zen said.

I slipped on my dress. "Yeah, I agree. There's something wrong there. Hawk didn't mention it, but then he got that info from his cop mole who could have slipped up. But neither did Bev. Surely she didn't know. Wonder why that info is being kept under wraps?"

"Maybe the cops are thinking it may have been a suicide too?"

"Or maybe the bro was lying, trying to create a smoke screen."

I pulled on my wig and adjusted it.

"I suppose that's possible." I turned to Zen. "How do I look?"

She stepped forward and slid the wig to the left. "There. Better."

"What was your take on the bro?" Zen asked as we passed a dumpster, me giving it a wide birth.

"Didn't like him."

"Bravo. I thought that wheelchair would make you instantly feel sorry for him."

I half-smiled. "Guess I'm getting better at being objective, huh?

We stepped into the bright sunshine.

"You're getting better, that's for sure."

I stopped in my tracks when a thought hit me. I squeezed Zen's arm. "But if there is no killer, if Hill *did* poison himself, why did we get shot at? And what about my porter theory?"

Zen linked her arm in mine. "Maybe it was a mistake. Maybe we just happened to be in the wrong place at the wrong time. Maybe your imagination made up the idea the guy was the same one." She pulled her arm out from mine and walked on a little further. "So we can shed these get-ups?"

We stared at each other, both most likely remembering the sound of the bullets. Sneaking a look behind us, we turned back around and shuffled down the street.

Our next person to question before going to the cops was Bev's daughter, Diane Johnson. She had said she would see us at noon over her lunch break at a nearby Friendly's. She worked as a paralegal for a lawyer. It was ten. I could use a cup of coffee. "We're meeting Diane Johnson a couple blocks from here."

"We'll ditch the clothes?"

"Ah, let's just leave them on. It's not like we'll be seeing Diane again after this interview. That is, if she isn't the killer."

Too distracted to call Uber, I raised my hand to hail a taxi.

38

Diane Johnson sat at a booth with a cup of coffee in front of her. She had bobbed brunette hair and a chiseled model-prefect face. When I looked into her intelligent eyes, I saw her mother. When she spoke, I heard her mother's lilting voice. She eyed us up and down. "Nice look for you two. Very becoming."

Super. She knew who we were even in these get-ups. Great.

We smiled as we settled in the booth.

Diane glanced at the clock. "I only have forty minutes," she said. "What is it you want to talk to me about? I know you've spoken more than once to my mom."

"As you might guess, we're trying to create a profile of your step-dad to help us find his killer."

The light in Diane's eyes dimmed. "I would think you'd have a clear picture by now. Words that describe him are: manipulative, homophobic, greedy, and egotistical. The world is a better place without him."

"Yes, we understand you two did not get along," I said.

"Get along? That's rich! We hated each other. If I'd thought of it, I would have sent that tea."

"Who do you think did that?"

"Many might think my mother. He couldn't have been more cruel to her, but she had come to her senses and was divorcing him."

I let her talk.

"Could have been someone he screwed over in a real estate deal (Yes, I knew about his secret company), or my uncle who he treated like an old entry carpet. There are many possibilities."

"Did you know that your step-dad had cancer?" I asked.

"Well, no, actually, I didn't." She set down her mug. "Cancer?"

"Yes, pancreatic."

"That's pretty much incurable, right? When did he find out?""

I nodded. "Shortly after your mom filed for divorce. We're wondering if your mom knew."

"No way! If she did, she would have informed me." She looked over my shoulder. "So, he would have died anyway without the tea."

I nodded again.

"How ironic."

"Do you think your step-dad had it in him to send himself that tea, knowing he was dying?"

"Like he poisoned himself, so someone would pay for his death?"

"Yeah, something like that," I said.

"Pfft. Sounds just like him—evil and controlling beyond his death. Sure, it's possible."

Zen who had begun to fidget, piped up. "We understand that your mom was already plannin' to remarry?"

211

Diane sipped her coffee, and then said, "Yes, unfortunately she's one of those women who has to have a man in the wings before she can leave a bad marriage."

"What do you think of the new fella?" Zen asked.

"Breece? Oh, he's way too young for her and probably more interested in her money, than her. But hey? Anything to get her away from Mr. Evil."

Zen's face reddened. I kicked her under the booth. She lowered her head and buttoned her lips.

"Ever occur to you that he might have sent that tea?" I asked.

"Yeah, that went through my mind, more because of Simon's crooked role in that deal in Florida than because he was in the way of Mom's money. Breece was real upset about the Florida thing. I really never understood why."

Zen apparently couldn't take the ill comments about Breece any longer. Her head shot up and she glared at Diane. "Do you really think Breece would put other members of your family at risk by sending poisonous tea that could be drunk by anyone your step-dad offered it too? You think Breece is that evil too?"

"Hah! Breece was well aware that Simon would never consider sharing any gift he received. The two of us used to joke about that trait of Simon's."

Wanting her take on something that didn't set right at Bev's interview, I asked, "Why did Simon accept the tea as safe? Since he had so many enemies, surely he would worry about poison."

"You mean my mom didn't tell you about the fight they had about him using her cat Dolly to test the leaves? That was quite a battle I can tell you. It went on for a week until Mom finally gave in."

"I got the impression your mom never stood up to Simon," I said.

"Oh, normally she didn't. But when I, Katie—my daughter—or Dolly were concerned, she was a real lion protecting her cubs."

"Yet, she gave in."

Diane's facial expression hardened. "Yes, she did."

"And the cat wasn't poisoned."

She stood. "Listen, must run. It's been fun."

After Diane left, Zen insisted she needed a double banana split to quell her anger. I started to protest. "This is an ice cream shop, ain't it?" she demanded.

I ordered a small pineapple sundae with jimmy's and extra nuts, my favorite. "I just had an icky thought."

"Yeah?" I licked my spoon.

"You don't suppose Bev would have it in her to switch cats, do you?"

I cringed. "Eww. How disgusting." No longer hungry, I set down my spoon. "No animal lover would do such a thing, right? Buy a sacrificial cat?"

"I heard worse," Zen said. "But the cat had no signs of being poisoned by the tea. Hill was poisoned by the tea."

"Yep. Something ain't right."

When we left the shop, Zen was still upset about Breece. Knowing our disguises weren't working, I suggested we head back to Mom's place to form a better plan. I didn't want to take the chance of going to the police station to report the porter just yet. Too risky. Zen refused to talk in the taxi. I paid and tipped the driver and we hurried up the steps. I was more than relieved when I realized no one was home. Zen hurried down the hallway. I assumed she was attempting to recover from her anger at what Diane had said about Breece.

Diane's words, for me, had put a whole new spin on things. I now wondered if Breece should be the No. 1 suspect. After all, he had a double motive, knew plenty about oleander and had knowledge of the family's quirks.

As I pulled off my wig in my room and combed my fingers through my hair, I wondered how we could prove it. My monkey ring went off. I grabbed for my iPhone. Sam. She was in the hospital. Her apartment had been ransacked and she had been knocked out cold. She gave me the name of the hospital and I said we'd be there ASAP.

"Zen, we've got to go. Sam's been hurt! Someone broke into her apartment," I yelled as I slammed the wig back on my head. "Keep your disguise on and hurry!" Our garb would just have to do for now. There was no time to think of another alternative.

I called Uber and a driver was out front in less than five minutes. As we ran down the steps I said, "God, I hope this had nothing to do with us!"

In the car Zen turned to me. "Uh, Jessie, there's something I need to tell you." She confessed about talking to Breece, about practically telling him where we were staying.

"Damn," I said.

"I'm sorry. I shouldn't have blabbed about it. After what Diane said, I started thinking that maybe Breece wasn't so innocent in this whole thing. And now this. Maybe that porter and Breece are working together. Maybe Breece contacted him after I called?"

"Yeah, maybe."

"So what should we do?" Zen asked.

"I wish I knew."

At the hospital, Sam assured us that the break-in had nothing to do with us. "It was a burglary," she said. "Nothing more. The assailant went through my stuff. Like, I have jewelry or clothing worth something! HAH!"

"Your oboe?" I said.

"Thank god, I left it at the theater."

Sam was released and we accompanied her home. All the way she apologized for bothering us, said she had to admit without family close, it was nice to have our support. We told her we were more than glad to take her home and stay with her if she wanted.

"I don't need a babysitter. In fact, I have a rehearsal this evening," she said.

"You sure you should go?" I asked.

"Absolutely."

We took Uber back to Mom's. Again, no one was there when we arrived.

Later, I thought I heard Grandma and Mom on the steps, so I opened the door. They were nowhere in sight.

A cool breeze brushed against my cheeks. I set my fear of being recognized aside. The white dusting gave everything a sense of peace. As if the snowflakes comforted the neighborhood—take a rest—stop worrying so much. I inhaled a deep breath. The breath, instead of settling me into a rational mode of thinking about the case, made me drift into a state that was close to meditation. My mind emptied. My eyes hardly registered the sights around me. A honking horn seemed a mile away. I took in air through my nose and exhaled through my mouth—again and again—breathing in a steady rhythm that felt comforting and welcoming and right.

"Jessie!! Whatever are you doing standing out in the open like that? Where is your disguise? What are you thinking?"

Mom. Damn.

"Hey, relax. The disguise was useless."

Mom dropped the grocery bag. "You're in the open like that knowing you're at risk of being shot? Did we raise you to act so thoughtless?"

"Hey, Mom, come on. That's what P.I.s do. You know that!! We lead dangerous lives. Besides, Zen and I decided those bullets were not meant for us." I'd go to confession later.

"But, you're an artist and a property manager! Oh, Jessie!"

I reached for the bag. "Mom, please!"

Her eyes filled with more fireworks and she stumbled up the steps, Grandma and I were right beside her. "If you'd only marry, you wouldn't have to do this," she hissed.

"Please, don't go there. PLEASE!!" Like my begging would stop her.

Grandma turned to her. "Jessie has always had a mind of her own, you know that, Edie." She patted her on the back. "Let's get inside." The aroma of baking meat drifted down the hall.

Inside, Grandma bolted all the locks, then glared at me before returning her attention to Mom. "Now, see, we're all safe and sound." She slipped off her coat, then said, "Edie, tell Jessie our good news."

Mom raised her head and sort of smiled, although her eyes were still laced in sparks. "Seeing you and thinking about what could have happened, well . . . Oh dear, I almost forgot." She pulled a tissue out of her dress pocket and blew her nose, then sniffled before looking at me. "Do you remember your old friend, Bahar? The girl who moved back to Iran?"

My heart fluttered so fast I thought I might faint. "Oh course. She was my best friend."

"She's coming for supper."

"What!?"

Mom was now a woman of purpose. When that happened, no one got in her way. "Yes, and I have a lot to do. The roast is in. We need to get these veggies ready and there's still the salad. Your grandma made her special cranberry salad too. Oh, I need to check my list. What if I forget something? Oh, dear!" She rushed down the hall toward the kitchen, calling over her shoulder, "Bahar moved back to the neighborhood a month ago. I couldn't believe my eyes when she came up to me in the grocery store."

I was having trouble taking in the news. "Bahar is here?"

Mom yelled over her shoulder. "Bahar and her husband will be here at 7. Ma, get in here and help me! Jessie, get out of those clothes."

Grandma patted my arm before hurrying away.

I stood in the center of the room, transfixed.

39

The doorbell rang. I was in shock overload. Bahar's sudden departure had left me with no closure after a traumatic incident and now thirteen years later, she was walking back into my life. What was I to say? How was I to act? How could I face the friend I had failed? Why did she want to see me? To spit on me?

Grandma rushed from the kitchen, wiping her hands on a towel draped from her belt. "That's them. Jessie, you come with me to the door. She's your friend."

I stepped away from the dining room table and hesitantly followed her to the door. She unbolted the locks. I gnawed on my lower lip. Ran my fingers through my hair. Straightened my shoulders.

Grandma swung the door open.

And there she was.

Not in a black chador as I had always imagined her. Not with a look of permanent pain marring her face. Not with fear-driven eyes.

No.

Long hair draped over shoulders. Eyes sparkling with warmth and humor. Reddened lips smiling. A white shirt revealing the curve of her breasts. Jeans tucked into ankle-length boots.

I couldn't stop blinking.

She held out her arms. Our eyes filled with tears. I stepped forward. It wasn't until her husband "uh, hummed" that we stepped apart.

Laughing, Bahar introduced Edward. We all hugged.

"Okay, young'uns, supper's ready," Grandma said. "Edie will throw a fit if her roast grows cold."

Grandma began the meal with the customary prayer of thanks. When she was finished, Mom handed the meat platter to Edward.

When the last serving plate was returned to the table, Mom turned to Bahar. "So, Bahar, dear, tell us what happened to you after leaving high school." Mom raised her fork and knife. "Jessie was so worried about you, but I guaranteed you were going to be fine. You were fine, weren't you?"

I bit my lower lip. Bahar's flipped her napkin and placed it on her lap. Edward shifted in his chair. Zen asked Grandma to pass the salt and pepper.

Bahar, moving her glass of water, leaned her head to the left and looked into Mom's eyes. "Well, I always missed Jessie, of course, but oh, my life has been charmed, Mrs. Murphy. It really has. After completing high school in Iran I travelled to Oxford, England for college. That's where I met Edward. We were mates all through undergrad and graduate school. My parents were relieved when we finally married." She laughed. "You know how parents are?"

Mom raised her chin and gave me an "I told you so" look I often gave Zen.

Bahar continued. "I'm a pediatrician. Edward's a heart surgeon. But enough about me. How have you all been?" She looked around the table.

Her words were like water spray at a car wash—me being the Chevy anxious to be free of road dirt.

To my surprise, Mom jumped in and grassed on and on about my art, my three jobs and my lifestyle of living both in Cambridge and Matlacha, explaining that I was staying with her and Grandma the short time I was in Boston since my apartment was rented out for the winter.

"We are so proud of Jessie," she ended, beaming at me.

Taken aback, I smiled back at her. Mom may lean toward the emotional shaky side, but she was my mom—a woman who never withheld her love. Grandma reached over and patted her hand.

Mahar winked at me. Zen nudged me on the shoulder. I grinned and shook my head.

After supper, while Edward helped in the kitchen, Bahar and I went to my bedroom in search of our junior yearbook. Zen said she was going to bed early. She was bushed.

Pulling the yearbook off the shelf, we sat on the edge of my bed with the book between us. I opened the cover, took a deep breath and said, "Bahar, what happened in that bathroom has always haunted me. I've always felt so badly I couldn't have done more to stop Roy."

The bathroom door across the hall opened. Bahar waited for it to close before answering.

"Hey, Mom got me counselling. Look at me. I'm more than fine."

"You didn't write. You didn't call," I said, leafing through the book.

221

"I know. Now I wish I had, but then, to be quite honest I was mad at you. You got to stay in America. As the years passed, I got over it, but it seemed too late for apologies."

I looked at her. "I've always envisioned you in a black chador."

"Yes, well, oh, sure, in Iran I had to wear one when I left the apartment, but once we moved to England I was free to wear what I wished and believe me I did and more. Look!"

She pulled down the edge of her shirt to reveal a tiny rose tattoo on her left shoulder.

"Ohmigod, Bahar, even I don't have a tat!"

We chuckled. Then needing to finish what I had started, I said, "Roy was killed in a car accident shortly after the, uh, incident."

"We heard. Fitting retribution, huh?"

I blinked several times. This was equally as bad of a tragedy—the death of those kids. "Two kids in the other car were killed. If I had only. . ." I choked back my tears.

Bahar put her arm around my shoulders and pulled me to her. "I know. I know. Listen, I'm the one who begged you not to tell. You can't blame yourself. If there is anyone to blame, it's me."

I let the tears stream down my face. Guilt had always been my albatross. The feeling almost destroyed me when my first love was murdered. I knew this. But knowing it and controlling it were not the same thing.

"Listen, Jessie, this may not help, but please know that it was because of those kids deaths I decided to become a pediatrician. Their young lives were taken away and that was a horrible tragedy. But good can come from evil. We must remember that."

After Bahar and her husband left, I was surprised at how relieved I felt. It was like she'd unloaded a ton of stone off my shoulders. Guilt had made me question my abilities as a P.I. Guilt had chipped away at my self-esteem.

I began to doodle. I drew Bahar in street clothes. Bahar in a doctor's office wearing a white jacket taking care of two little girls. Bahar smiling. A rose tattoo. Bahar with windswept hair smiling at Edward, me standing in the background. Minute by minute I felt my confidence returning. So what if I wasn't perfect? Perfection was over-rated.

Steeled to take on the world again—or at least a killer who knew a lot about oleander—I stood, walked to my window and pulled back my curtain. Almost lost in the shadows, a beefy man in a long dark coat leaned against the building across the street.

With tears of relief flowing, I waved at him.

40

It was good to be back. I sometimes wondered what made some people fully content to remain in one location while others like me needed more diverse place stimuli. It's funny, I hadn't known this about myself until Will's death had brought me down to Florida, but as soon as I realized that I actually could make two living places work for me—I went for it.

Zen was anxious to be home as well. When I dropped her off at her trailer and conveyed to her the news that we should go to Arcadia the next day, her disappointment was evident.

By this point, we were pretty well convinced that Breece was the killer and that the porter was a hired accomplice.

I was sure there were answers to be had in Arcadia. Answers that would help end the case.

The next morning, after taking my power walk, I made out an expense statement for Shirin's cousin, then spent the day researching details about George Voss and Diane Johnson. Even though both of them had a motive for murder, their information didn't lead me to think they were the killers. Turns out Voss was up for the position of CEO since last spring as Hill had planned to step down. Diane might have hated Hill, but she didn't come across as a killer (and, no, I didn't feel sorry for her).

The most important information I got from our Boston trip was the realization that we were being tailed by the "porter"—a fact that was unsettling. I also reminded myself that I'd never contacted the Boston police, promising myself I would take care of that detail after going to Arcadia. On a personal level, I'd say it was more significant seeing and talking with Bahar. That meeting was a life changer for me—a welcomed life changer.

Arcadia was a small inland town with Main Street antique stores, tourist shops, and places to eat. Richard Rancine lived one block north on a parallel street in a Victorian house surrounded by at least an acre of land brimming with lush landscape.

"Someone's master gardening skills show." I shifted gears and parked in the driveway.

"Yeah, sweet," Zen said.

I turned to her. "You didn't tell anyone where we were going, right?"

"Nah, I learned my lesson."

"Good. I don't think we were followed. Listen, I'm planning to show him a group of sketches of our people of interest. I want you to use your poker skills and watch his face and body language to see if you think he's lying. Can you do that?"

"Are you kiddin'? That's one of my specialties."

Of course it was. I clutched my sketchpad. "Okay, let's go. He's expecting us."

The property was lined with a fifteen foot high fence of oleander in full bloom. Each plant displayed different color blossoms. When Zen saw them, she poked my arm with her elbow and raised and lowered her eyebrows quickly.

"Yeah, I see. He could poison an army with all this," I said in a low voice.

I knocked. The door was opened by a short, balding man who wore frameless, thick-lensed glasses. His round, chubby face and neck were surprisingly chalk white. Apparently he used lots of sunscreen. The knees of his jeans were soiled, as were his work gloves. I knew from my research that he was a sixty-seven-year-old former accountant with no police record, served on the Arcadia town council, had been married thirty years, and had no siblings and no debt.

We introduced ourselves and he led us to a living room furnished in period pieces.

"Your call intrigued me," Rancine said. "I'm not used to having people interested in my gardening habits. Are you writing an article? Please sit." He motioned to the sofa, taking a high-backed chair. I sat, but Zen, hands clasp behind her, walked around the room.

"No, and I apologize for not explaining the reason for our visit. I thought it best said in person. We're investigating the murder of a man and your name came up."

"Really? How dreadful. So much violence today. What's the name of this unfortunate fellow?"

Zen stopped walking and faced him.

"Simon Hill."

Rancine's right eye twitched ever so slightly. "Hmm, Hill. Why, no. I'm afraid I never knew him. Is he from Arcadia?"

I leaned back on the sofa. "No, he was a snowbird from Boston who had a home in Matlacha."

"I see. Well I've never been to Matlacha and the last time I was in Boston was over ten years ago. I took my wife there on vacation. Great city, but too bustling for us. We were glad to get home."

Zen stepped backward.

"Do you know a man named Breece Devino?"

"Breece? Why, yes. He's one of my hybrid suppliers. He always has quality stock." His expression went grim. "I do hope he's not involved in the murder?"

"Please, if you don't mind, let me ask the questions."

The light in his eyes dimmed, but he nodded and pushed his glasses up the bridge of his nose.

I warned myself to not get on his bad side. Charm, Jessie. Be charming, not confrontational.

I leaned forward and smiled. "I'm sorry about that last comment. As you might guess we can't divulge facts about our case."

His face relaxed and I continued. "I assume you're aware that oleander leaves are potentially dangerous to humans and animals?"

"Of course, but only if ingested."

"The man was killed by oleander poisoning."

Rancine shot up straight in the chair. "Oh, I see. And since I grow a wide variety of oleander and my name came up, as you say, then you think I could be the murderer? How preposterous!"

"Please, don't make that assumption. This is merely a lead we're following, nothing else." I let that sink in. "We're working hard at remaining objective."

"I see. How can I help you?"

"What can you tell us about Breece Devino?"

"All I know is that he has an herbalist background, plays some kind of musical instrument and manages to supply me with the variety of oleander that satisfies my wants."

"How did you first meet him?"

"Through an ad in the newspaper."

"Does he bring the stock to you?"

"Yes, he does."

"Has he always come alone?"

"Always."

"Does the name Shirin Raad ring a bell?"

"Not at all. Sounds middle eastern."

Rancine cocked his head. I nodded to Zen. She positioned herself in full view of him.

I withdrew my sketchpad from my backpack. Opening it, I flipped through the pages. "Do you recognize this woman?" It was Shirin.

"No."

I turned another page. "This one?" Shirin's cousin.

"No."

Another page.

"This guy?"

"Sure, that's Breece. Good likeness."

I smiled in lieu of a thank you, turned a page and held up the book again. "This?" Simon Hill.

His left eye twitched before he said no.

I continued. "This?" Beverly Hill.

"No."

"This woman?" Moon McCain.

"No."

"This one?" Paul Lowinski.

He looked at the floor. I glanced toward Zen. She was in full attention.

"No."

I continued. "This?" The porter.

"No."

"One more." I turned the page and held up the book. Lester Hill.

Slight pause. "No."

I closed the sketchbook. "Well that's it. Thanks for your co-operation. It's really appreciated."

We went toward the door.

"Hey, do you mind if we walk around your yard? It's so cool with all the plants and stuff. I can see why you thought we might be writin' an article. This place deserves to be in a magazine. Don't you think so, Jessie?"

I agreed and Rancine grinned. He said we were more than welcome to take a look. He had a council meeting in fifteen minutes so had to leave.

Outside, he went to the detached garage, soon reversed in an SUV and waved as he left. Zen wagged her Stetson.

"So, what do you think?" I asked.

"He lied about knowing Simon Hill, Paul Lowinski and maybe Lester Hill."

"The eye twitch was his tell, right?"

"Oh, yeah."

"That's what I thought."

"You know what's out back?" she asked.

"What?"

"A motorhome."

"So? They like to camp."

"Yeah, but maybe it's something else," Zen said.

"Like what?"

"Like a mobile meth lab."

"Hey!" I said with raised eyebrows. "I'm the one who's supposed to have the over-active imagination."

Zen chuckled. "Well, I'm curious, even if you ain't."

I shrugged. "Okay, okay, let's take a look."

We came to a wall of areca palms. "How'd you see it anyway? It's hidden behind these damn things." I slid my hand into a thick growth to see if I could find a hole to walk through. No luck. I wandered further down the wall.

Zen was doing the same. "Yeah, that's what made me curious. Could only see the top of it. Of course might be hiding it so they don't have to see it when they're not camping—damn!"

"What!?"

"Rat just ran across my boot."

"Oh, shit!" I had on flip flops. EEK!

"Rats love arecas. Here's an opening. Come on!"

We rushed through, coming out into a clearing where the thirty-foot or so motorhome was parked. Its window blinds were closed. We hurried to the door. "Padlocked," Zen said.

I pulled out a handy tool I always carry from my pocket, hunkered down and did my P.I. 101 magic. The lock popped.

"Oh god, you're a queen," Zen said. "I really need to learn how to do that."

I winked at her, opened the door and went up the two steps. "Whoa! Stay out there!"

"What?"

"It's not safe in here. Stay there."

The room was filled with large cooking pots, gas canisters, tubes, thermostats and stacks of plastic bags in boxes. A protective mask and suit was draped over a chair. I pulled out my phone and took several photos. Inhaling and wishing I hadn't, I clamped my hand over my mouth and nose. "This place is contaminated, step back. Let me out!"

Pushing Zen backward, I rushed down the steps, slammed the door shut and fastened the padlock, wiping my fingerprints off the handle and lock. "Let's get out of here before someone shows up!" I said.

"A lab?"

"Oh, yeah. Big time."

We hurried through the clearing, the arecas and to my car.

I slid behind the steering wheel. "You call in an anonymous tip while I drive." I tossed my phone in Zen's lap, then had an idea. "No, wait."

"What?" Zen said.

"We want to catch our killer, right?"

"Sure."

"Okay, let's get out of here first."

We were less than a mile down the road when my plan finalized. "Okay, here's what I'm thinking. We need to stake out the place. See who comes and goes."

"Hey, these type of scum are dangerous, kiddo," Zen said. "I vote for gettin' the place busted and lettin' the chips fall where they may."

"How would that lead to our killer's door?"

"I don't know, but I do know that people who deal in meth aren't the type to take highly to two females spyin' on them. I ain't willin' to get killed for the price of a TV set."

I looked long and hard at Zen. Something else was bothering her. That was obvious. A car came towards us. Headlights blinked. I lowered mine. "You're right. I'll make the call from my room."

"I think we should consider ourselves damn lucky. If anyone had seen us, I don't even want to think."

We drove back to Matlacha in thoughtful silence.

I dropped Zen off at her place promising to call her in the morning.

I pulled down my Stetson and hunkered down, grabbing two planted pork and bean cans. Wham! Wham! The cans, the plants, the dirt smashed against the wall and splattered on the floor. Second hand loads followed the first. Wham! Wham! So you like to give oleander, do you? Well, here's my gift to you! Wham! Wham! Wham! Wham! Again and again and again I grabbed and threw not caring what the can knocked over. Breathing heavily, I threw my Stetson on the floor, reached in my purse and pulled out my girdle and a pair of scissors and with relish cut it into tiny little pieces that I dropped inside my hat. When finished, I flipped the Stetson high into the air, letting the contents fall—little turds released from a crazed falcon. A bucket filled with water sat under a window. My eyes narrowed. I smiled and walked that way.

When I got back to the room, I changed into a black, long-sleeved shirt and black jeans, then tucked my hair under a black cap.

I was back in Arcadia just after nightfall. I parked three miles away behind a no longer operating gas station I'd seen as we left town earlier. Opening the trunk, I took out a flashlight, my revolver, handcuffs and bug spray. After applying a generous amount of spray, I hunched my shoulders and began the trek to Rancine's house. No one was about. I saw

233

no curtains or blinds raise and lower. When I got near his property I saw that someone was inside. Several rooms were lit downstairs. I hunkered down and using the arecas and oleander bushes as cover, ran toward the motorhome. Spreading out the camping blanket I carried in my pocket amidst a bank of areca palms, I stretched out on the ground, got comfy and began my surveillance.

I totally agreed with Zen, there was no reason she should put herself at risk. I was the boss. The one who should shoulder the responsibility. And, thanks to Bahar, my shoulders felt real strong right now, hefty.

Things get boring when you're waiting, but what kept me alert was knowing that rats loved arecas. Minutes ticked away and away and away. Just as I was thinking no one would show up, I heard voices. I flattened against the ground.

"Hurry up and unlock that door. I don't want to be seen out here." It was Breece.

"Hold on. There, got it."

"Where the hell is Rancine? He's always on time."

"Don't know, but get in." The door shut.

Assuming Rancine would be coming soon, I stayed put. Within seconds I heard footsteps. Rancine. He opened the door, climbed the steps and disappeared inside. I could only hear muffled voices.

Gun drawn, inch-by-inch I crawled closer. The voices became more distinct.

"Listen, goat heads," Breece growled. "After tonight, I'm out of this. I didn't bargain for no murder."

"No one is getting out," Rancine said. "No one. We're in this together!"

Scuffling. Glass breaking. A louder crash. The door flew open. Breece, with bloodied lip, filled the doorway, carrying a gas canister. I was totally exposed. He saw me and ran forward, the canister over his head. I barely had time to take aim.

Bam! Bam!

Breece fell. The canister rolled to the side.

Stunned, because I hadn't fired, I looked toward the door. Rancine, blood dripping down his face, his glasses askew, stood in the doorway, a revolver in his hand, the barrel aimed at my head.

I raised my gun.

BAM!

Rancine went to his knees then tumbled down the steps.

Puzzled, I looked at my still unfired gun, then into the sky and whispered, "Thank you."

"You, in there. Put your hands over your head and get out here. If you have a revolver kick it out the door first," a woman's voice demanded.

Lowinski, in a white suit, white headgear and blue gloves, hands over his head, stood in the doorway.

"Keep those arms high. Murphy, get up and go get that gun," the same voice said.

My eyes were now so wide you could fit a sauce plate in the sockets if they were empty. My heart thundered like the beat of an escaping iguana.

"Murphy, get up. You're safe now. We got `em."

Still unable to stand, I managed to turn my head to stare at the Amish women and the porter.

Looking disgusted, the porter walked forward, reached down and began to pull me up. "Those guys scared the bejesus out of you, huh?"

I nodded my head to indicate he should look to my right.

"Good god!" he yelled.

Raising his Glock, he pulled the trigger. One foot away a rat the size of a cat toppled over. I let out the breath I'd been chewing on and began sobbing and laughing hysterically.

Bam!

The porter went down on one knee then collapsed on top of the rat.

Bam! Bam!

Bodies fell behind me.

In a flash, I rolled to the left, then aimed. This time my gun fired and Coconut Paul Lowinski, still holding a gun, screamed and fell onto his knees. I fired again. His face bit the dirt.

41

Ah, the Community Park. Salty breeze. Dolphins playing offshore. Pelicans soaring low. Sandpipers scurrying across broken seashells. What's not to love?

"Hey, let's play Frisbee!" Ter, the undercover agent yelled.

"Too much work," I called back.

Ter's partner, Heather, jumped up. "I'll play! Come on, you islanders. Don't be lazy butts. Florida fried your energy?"

"Let's see who's a lazy butt!" Zen jettisoned to her feet and headed toward Ter, cartwheeling all the way.

Ter laughed and threw the Frisbee. Heather caught it, swiveled and flipped it toward me.

I snatched it and stood. I mean, really! One really should jump at challenges. My toss resembled a planet spinning in full cinque with its orbit.

The game went on for more than half an hour. Sweating, we dove into the water before dashing to our blankets, applying new sunscreen, and then stretching out.

I sighed heavily. "So glad Ty is recouping."

"Yeah. He was lucky. The bullet missed his knee cap by barely an inch."

Zen bent her elbow and placed her head on her hand, smiling at the agents. "Not that you two weren't lucky. Here, Here for your bullet-proof vests."

"Yeah, but you ever been hit with a bullet at that range, even with a vest on? We both went down like sacks of potatoes. Lucky for us, that's when your friend here took over."

Zen gave me a wink. "Of course. This girl can act and act fast."

I gave Zen a "hah" look and turned onto my stomach.

"How long were you watching the ring?" I asked, eyes half-closed.

"For over a year. Devino was a new add-on. Hill, Lowinski and Rancine were the initial key players."

"So why did they kill Hill?"

"That's the funny thing, they didn't."

"What?" I said, sitting up.

"Oh, they thought they had. Rancine had the oleander tea leaves delivered, but Hill died of cancer. A fact we kept under wraps."

"He didn't die of poison?"

"Nah, pancreatic cancer."

"Damn! But why keep that information from his wife?"

"Oh, she knew, but she agreed to go along with the poison story."

"Why?" I said.

"We hoped them thinking they'd murdered Hill might serve as glue to keep the scumbags together until we could make a valid arrest. We figured Devino would want to split soon, him going to marry Bev Hill and all," Ter said.

"Was that *really* in the cards," Zen asked.

"Nah, no chance," Heather said. "Bev Hill suspected him from the get-go of only wanting her money and she told us so. She knew he was a drug addict and probably worse.

"Those creeps have been hauling the motorhome lab around southern Florida for some time now. Every time we got close, it disappeared again. These guys were no dummies."

"Yeah, and thanks to you, we found it and were able to nail them."

"And how did Shirin Raab fit into this?" A lightbulb went off. "You two knew all along she'd hadn't murdered Hill, because he wasn't murdered."

"Bingo!"

"She was working undercover for us. While she was in prison. Lowinski used to visit her dying inmate, his sister. He made the mistake of confiding in her. Since the sister thought her cellmate would never be paroled and was too shy to talk, she often bent Raab's ear. After the sister died, Raab had the warden contact us and cut a deal—her freedom for information that would break a meth ring."

"It was a simple plan," Heather said. "We had her contact Rancine with an offer to be one of his distributors. She used the sister connection to gain their trust. When he demanded proof of their friendship, she mailed him a book the sister had given her in prison—one that Lowinski had given her.

"Aha. Thus the package sent to Arcadia and the Arcadia trip."

"Precisely."

239

"Did she know that Hill was the one who raped her?"

"Not until that day on the train. That made her all the more determined to get them. He was the Boston connection for a very lucrative business. She was as surprised as we were when he died."

I gazed out over the water. "So, all along Shirin knew that you knew she was innocent of killing Hill?"

"Yep."

"And why did her cousin hire us?"

"To get you involved. We knew that Zen and Devino played poker together and we knew you used her as a sidekick. We thought those two might even be having an affair. We knew Bev and he were. That Bev Hill has a wild side, that's for sure. With you two serving as P.I.s, we felt if we followed you, you might lead us to the meth. And you did."

"What about the fight on the dock?"

"Devino started that. We had approached him about buying some meth. He met us at the beach. But for some reason we never knew, he got suspicious and well, you saw what happened. We were glad you came along. We weren't ready to blow our cover yet."

"You used us from Day One?" Zen said, wide-eyed.

"Afraid so."

Zen pouted. I'd already done my pouting on that score.

"So, who shot at us in Boston?" I asked.

"Our guess is that you were in the wrong place at the wrong time. Another theory is that Breece Devino and the crew hired someone to get rid of you. So far they haven't admitted to that."

Zen's eyes teared. She stood and walked to the shoreline.

"Too bad. She liked him, didn't she?" Heather said.

"Yeah, she's getting over it in her own way. She's also really upset with herself that she didn't realize I would go back to Arcadia that night."

"We all make mistakes. Sorry payment for the job didn't work out."

"Yeah, well, whatever."

"What do you hear about Bev Hill?' Heather asked.

"Apparently she and her daughter are taking mindfulness classes. You know—yoga and meditation."

"With gurus?"

Still thinking about Zen and how bad she must be feeling, I nodded. "Seems Bev has the hots for hers. Rumor has it that she confessed to him that she sacrificed a cat in the name of justice. The guru assured her that all bad karma would be erased if she donated fifty thousand dollars to his institute. The money was transferred the next day. The guru is Zen's yoga instructor."

Zen put her hands on the ground, straightened her legs and pushed her butt into the air, executing a downward dog pose. After holding for several seconds, she lowered herself into a plank position.

"That girl knows her yoga moves," Heather said. "I hear the annexation issue is still up for grabs."

"Yeah, I heard that too."

As the tide came in, Zen pushed upward, bent her right knee—toes forward, left leg extended behind her—toes pointing to the side, and

241

stretched out her arms—one forward, one back. Head facing right fingertips. Water sliding toward her feet.

"Nice warrior pose," Heather called to her.

Zen turned her head. "Don't forget," she yelled. "I'm still savin` for that 52-inch flat screen. Count me in for the next case!"

ACKNOWLEGMENTS

The author wishes to acknowledge the invaluable assistance and support of the following writers and editors: Marjorie Carlson Davis, Claudia Bischoff, Suzanne Kelsey, Jeannette Batko, Barbara Darling, Faith Gansheimer and Ellen Larson. A special thanks goes to friend Sherry Sgkochanski who spent hours emailing libraries and who is her all-important Florida walking buddy and confidante. She would also like to thank her beloved family and the business owners of Matlacha for always having her back.

ABOUT THE AUTHOR

jd daniels lives and writes both in Florida and Iowa. She lived in the Boston area when her children were preschoolers. She holds a Doctor of Arts degree from Drake University and since the mid-eighties has taught at the college level. She enjoys travel, kayaking, bicycling, bridge and mahjong. Even more, she likes laughing and sharing stories with friends and family.

Her Website: **www.live-from-jd.com**

OTHER BOOKS BY THE AUTHOR

JESSIE MURPHY MYSTERIES

Through Pelican Eyes

Quick Walk to Murder

Mayhem in Matlacha

STAND ALONE NOVELS

Minute of Darkness & Eighteen Flash

Fiction Stories

NONFICTION

The Old Wolf Lady: A Biography

(First Edition)

The Old Wolf Lady: Wawewa Mepemoa

(Second Edition)

POETRY

Currents that Puncture: A Dissertation

Say Yes

www.ingramcontent.com/pod-product-compliance
Lightning Source LLC
Chambersburg PA
CBHW022002170626
46808CB00001B/258